"You think you are irresistible."

India was bitterly angry but realized she had gone too far when she saw the gleam in his eyes.

"Want me to prove I am?" There was seduction in the soft words. She made no demur as his arms came around her, her eyes wide open and her body quivering tensely as she waited for his kiss. But instead of possessing her mouth, his lips were exploring the contours of her face, his thumbs slowly stroking the soft flesh of her throat, until she ached with the tension of denying her body's response. It took all her willpower to keep from turning her head to meet his lips. Her mouth felt dry, her heart thudding against her ribs.

Then, when she had ceased to expect it, his mouth closed over hers, and a strange feeling spread slowly throughout her body.

PENNY JORDAN

an unbroken marriage

Harlequin Books

TORONTO • NEW YORK • LOS ANGELES • LONDON
AMSTERDAM • PARIS • SYDNEY • HAMBURG
STOCKHOLM • ATHENS • TOKYO • MILAN

Harlequin Presents first edition December 1982
ISBN 0-373-10553-3

Original hardcover edition published in 1982
by Mills & Boon Limited

CHAPTER ONE

'MELISANDE's here—and you should see the man she's got with her!' Jennifer Knowles announced, walking into her employer's work-room and rolling her eyes expressively. 'Gorgeous—and rich too, by the looks of him. Well, if he's Melisande's latest, he'll need to be, won't he?' she added forthrightly. 'I didn't realise we had anything in hand for her. What is it, there's nothing in the book.' She frowned a little as she studied the leather-bound book India used to book in and chart the progress of her orders. 'We finished the black silk last week.'

'Umm,' India Lawson agreed, removing half a dozen pins from her mouth and studying the pink silk blouse she was working on. 'She's been invited to a Charity Ball—she rang me yesterday and asked if we could make something for her in a hurry.'

'Provided you let her have it at next to no cost,' Jennifer added caustically. 'Honestly, she's the limit! She must be earning a fortune from that part she landed in *Evergreen*. It's been running for six months now, and there's no sign of bookings dropping—I know, I tried to get seats for my mother and sister for next weekend.'

India smiled. 'Well, don't forget that simply by wearing our clothes Melisande is doing an excellent public relations job for us.'

'You're far too easygoing,' Jennifer scolded. 'I don't know how you do it; and you with auburn hair as well.'

5

India laughed. 'Tell Melisande I'll be with her in five minutes, would you Jen—oh, and offer her ...' She had been about to say a 'cup of coffee', but changed her mind, remembering her secretary's description of the actress's companion. 'Offer them a glass of sherry,' she corrected. 'I can't leave this blouse until I get these tucks right. I promised Lady Danvers that I'd have it ready for the weekend.'

The expressive line of Jennifer's departing back said what she thought of the way India, as she put it, 'pandered' to her clients' wishes, but then she did not have the responsibility of a business resting on her shoulders, India reflected.

Of course she enjoyed being her own boss, it had been her ambition since the Fifth Form at school when she had spent her Saturday mornings studying the shoppers in their often drab and ill-fitting clothes mentally re-clothing them in her own designs.

Not that it had been easy, but then those things really worth having rarely were, she decided. She had spent three years at art college, followed by another three in Paris working in a very lowly capacity for one of the well-known couturiers. After that there had been a spell on the buying side, learning about merchandising, stocking control, and a whole host of other vitally important things which sometimes got overlooked—to their cost—by those who thought 'artistic' genius enough to guarantee them success.

And it had all paid off. A small legacy from a great-uncle had provided her with enough capital to risk going it alone. To her delight her first very limited range of skirts and blouses had sold, enabling her to take the risk of leasing more expensive premises close enough to the heart of London to be called 'exclusive', and now she numbered among her clientele enough socially-conscious women for her designs to be becoming featured in glossy magazines and society columns.

Even so, it paid to keep one's feet on the ground, which was why India made no demur when women such as Melisande Blake, a well-known actress, insisted on being given a 'discount' on clothes which they were going to wear in public.

India smiled wryly as she put the blouse aside and stood up, studying her reflection in the small mirror behind her desk. So Jennifer thought she didn't have a temper. If only she knew! It was not so much that she didn't have one; more that over the years she had learned for her own sake to keep it strictly under control, although even now there were occasions when it suddenly and unexpectedly flared into all-consuming life.

Having checked that there were no threads clinging to her grey flannel skirt, India gave her reflection a final cursory glance before walking towards the door.

A short corridor linked the workrooms to the salon proper and when she opened the connecting door the first person she saw was the man whom her secretary had described as 'gorgeous'. She hadn't lied, India acknowledged, schooling her features into a professional smile, while inwardly noting the expensive cut of the pearl grey suit, the toning silk shirt and tie, the well manicured but entirely masculine hands, deeply tanned even though it was March, thick dark hair curling over his collar, his eyes a disturbing, deep blue.

'India darling!' Melisande greeted her in her husky, carrying voice. 'You've saved my life! Do show me what you have in mind. It must be something special—very special. If Simon likes it he's promised to buy me another. Will he like it?' she asked, adding mockingly, 'Really, darling, isn't it time you stopped wearing that frightful schoolgirl outfit? No one looking at you would have the faintest idea that you design the most incredibly sexy dresses!'

India thought she had been quite successful in hiding her reaction to hearing her clothes described in such a fashion until she glanced up and found Melisande's companion watching her with mocking comprehension.

'Oh, I haven't introduced you, have I?' the actress said. 'Simon darling, this is India, she really is the cleverest thing. India, meet Simon Herries—you must have read about him in the gossip columns.'

'I have, and in the financial press.' India agreed lightly, conscious of the sudden alertness in Simon Herries' expression.

'You take a keen interest in the world of big business, then?'

Gritting her teeth át the condescending tone, India replied lightly, 'Of course—what female doesn't in one form or another?'

She could tell from his expression that her barb had found its mark. He was far too intelligent to have imagined that Melisande's interest in him was purely altruistic, but, India thought shrewdly, he was attractive enough for it to wound his vanity to be told that others were aware of the fact too.

She had known Melisande for several years, and while the actress made no secret of the fact that she expected her escorts to be presentable and sexually attractive, she also expected them to be wealthy enough to afford her.

India watched her, aware of the contrast they must present. Melisande, small, barely five foot three, with fair, almost silver hair, and prettily feminine features—the archetype of female beauty, while she. . . . She wrinkled her nose slightly. She was tall, five eight in her stockinged feet; her hair, as Jenny had remarked, was a deep, intense auburn, saved from being unkindly described as 'red' by rich russet undertones; her green eyes set slightly aslant beneath well defined eyebrows, only her vulnerably full mouth betraying the fact that she was less self-possessed than first appeared.

She knew that Simon Herries was watching her, and she strove to fight off the inclination to return his look. She could almost feel his eyes sliding down her body, resting on the unexpectedly full curves of her breasts, the slimness of her waist, and the slender length of her legs.

His eyes rested on her legs for several seconds, a thoughtful, appraising look in them when he finally raised them to India's faintly flushed face.

'Quite an enigma,' he remarked softly. 'Prissy blouse, schoolgirl skirt and silk stockings.'

'It isn't meant to be,' India assured him with a calmness she was far from feeling—there had been something in the look he had given her which had sent vague frissons of awareness running down her spine. It wasn't unusual for her clients to bring men along with them—sometimes to pay, sometimes merely to approve, and she was used to the flirtatious, sometimes almost offensive comments some of them made, but this was something different; something alien and almost frightening; an absurd awareness of her own femininity which had nothing to do with the conversation and everything to do with the way had looked at her, and how her body had reacted to it.

'Oh, India is far from prissy, as I have very good reason to know,' Melisande remarked archly. 'I happen to know that she has a very charming and extremely wealthy boy-friend. In fact she brought him to my last party, didn't you, darling? Melford Taylor,' she added for Simon Herries' benefit, mentioning the name of a well-known financier.

Although India wasn't looking at him, she could feel Simon Herries appraising the salon with fresh eyes. It was decorated in white and gold with touches of green, sharp and fresh, and yet with an unmistakable richness. India had designed it herself, and the alterations and decorations had been carried out by a small firm specialising in stage settings. With ingenuity and flair the work had cost very little in terms of actual money, and India had repaid the help she had had from her friends by recommending them whenever she could. Some of the stage settings for Melisande's latest play had been designed by them, but because she very rarely allowed her private and business lives to mingle she doubted if Melisande was even aware that she knew them. She had only attended the party Melisande had mentioned because the actress had insisted upon it, and yet India could tell that Simon Herries was assessing the cost of the salon; that he could probably gauge the rental on it to the nearest pound, and was quite obviously thinking that Mel had paid for it.

India was no naïve young girl. She was twenty-five and had lived alone since the death of her parents when she was twenty. She was perfectly well aware of the moral code prevailing in the circles in which Melisande and presumably Simon Herries himself moved; and the conclusions he had undoubtedly drawn from Melisande's reference to Mel, and she longed to refute them. She and she alone was responsible for her success. She had received no financial 'help' or reward from other people, and she bitterly resented the implication that she was the sort of woman who chose the men in her life for what she could gain from the relationship.

Which was quite ridiculous, she told herself as she went to unlock the discreetly concealed floor-to-ceiling cupboards in which she kept completed orders. Why should it matter to her if Simon Herries judged her as he himself was no doubt quite happy to be judged? Her relationship with Melford Taylor was her own business and no one else's. Except of course that Mel happened to be married, she reminded herself wryly, as she removed the pale blue satin dress from its hanger.

'I love the colour,' Melisande enthused. 'Darling, I really must insist that you design my wardrobe for my next role. You know I've landed the female lead in *The Musgraves*?'

India inclined her head in acknowledgment.

'It was Simon who clinched things for me really,' Melisande added, scarlet-tipped nails almost stroking the grey-suited arm resting on the chair next to her own. 'He has extensive interests in commercial TV.'

'Really?'

India was not aware quite how dampening she had made the word sound until she looked up and caught the grey eyes watching her with curt anger. She had already heard that Melisande had got the main role in the proposed new TV blockbuster series, but stage costume designing was unfamiliar territory to her, and while she appreciated Melisande's faith in her, she felt that she had more than enough on her hands with the salon. The sudden boom in 'high living' had meant that she had had to take on extra staff to cope with the orders as it was, and she was cautious about who she employed.

'I'm sure he'll put in a good word for you with the studio bosses,' Melisande said.

'I'm sure Miss Lawson doesn't need me to help her, not with Melford Taylor as her . . . backer.'

Fighting down the sudden surge of anger which had almost taken her unawares, India turned her back on him, glad of the excuse of suggesting to Melisande that she help her with the dress. It was years since she had felt such an almost immediate antipathy towards someone, even given that she was being quite deliberately needled. And why, she could not imagine! Even if she were Mel's mistress, to use an outdated word, what possible business was it of Simon Herries?

In the fitting room she helped Melisande on with the blue satin. The bodice was cleverly draped to flatter the actress's figure, with the pencil-slim skirt which India knew she favoured.

'It's gorgeous!' Melisande pronounced when she had finished studying her reflection.

'The hem has to be finished and one or two other

little things done, but you'll have it tomorrow,' India
promised.

She could hear her private phone ringing and
sighed, knowing that it would be Mel. She had told
him last weekend that there was no future in their
relationship. She liked him; he had a good sense of
humour and was a pleasant, undemanding companion, but as she had pointed out to him, he *was* a
married man.

Hadn't she heard of divorce? Mel had asked her
quizzically, but India had cut him short. He had, as
she knew, two small children, and even if she had
been in love with him, which she wasn't, she doubted
if she could have brought herself to be the one responsible for depriving them of their father. The
reason was quite simple; during her own childhood
her father had had an affair with another woman. It
had lasted about a year. India had been twelve at
the time, a very impressionable age. She had known
that something was wrong. Her mother and father
never seemed to laugh any more, and she had caught
her mother crying. It hadn't been long before an
older, more knowing child at school had enlightened
her. She could remember quite vividly the sickness
which had overwhelmed her; the need to be alone,
to be assured that what she had heard wasn't true.
She had gone home and poured out the whole thing
to her mother. It was true, her mother had explained, but that didn't mean Daddy no longer loved
her. He did, very much.

Her mother had been extremely courageous, India
reflected, thinking about that time now. It couldn't
have been easy, trying not to let her own doubts and
bitterness affect India's relationship with her father,

but somehow she had succeeded, and been rewarded, when eventually the affair had fizzled out. Afterwards neither of her parents made any reference to what had happened, and to all intents and purposes lived quite amicably together, but the experience had changed India, made her question life and love far more deeply than most girls of her age, and although she was reluctant to admit it, had made her wary and mistrustful, unconsciously unwilling to commit herself to any deep emotional involvement with a man so that somehow, at twenty-five she had emerged from her teens and early twenties without the sexual and emotional experience most girls of her age took for granted.

When they returned to the salon Simon Herries was studying a seascape hanging on one of the walls. India's father had painted it before his death, and it depicted the view from their Cornish home on the cliffs high above the Atlantic. It was from her father that she had inherited the ambition which had made her successful, India acknowledged. He had been a civil engineer before his retirement, often working abroad. She herself had been conceived during a brief visit her mother had paid him when he was working on a contract in India—hence her unusual name.

'Cornwall?' he commented to India without lifting his eyes.

'Yes.'

'Your secretary came to look for you. She asked me to tell you that there'd been a call for you. Said you'd know who it was from.' This time he did look at her. 'It can't be easy, conducting an affair with a married man. You're to be congratulated. You've obviously been very discreet.'

He made it sound on a par with earning a living as a prostitute! Even Melisande caught the contemptuous undertone and frowned slightly.

'Oh, really, darling,' she protested, 'aren't you being just the tiniest bit old-fashioned? Extra-marital affairs are the norm these days. Be honest now, if you were married could you see yourself being faithful for the rest of your life? No, I think India has the right idea. Far better to be independent; to have a lover rather than a husband. You will make sure the dress is sent round tomorrow, won't you?' she asked India as Simon Herries helped her on with her fox jacket. 'Simon is taking me to the charity do at the Dorchester and I want to look my best.'

India walked with them to the door. Melisande kissed her on the cheek; she half extended her hand expecting Simon Herries to shake it formally, but to her chagrin he ignored her hand, instead glancing curtly down the length of her body, before following Melisande out to the sleek dark green Ferrari parked outside the salon.

'Umm, I wish I could find myself someone like that,' Jennifer commented dreamily, unashamedly watching them depart. 'Fantastic looks, money—and I'll bet he rates ten out of ten as a lover as well!'

'You'd probably be very disappointed,' India said briefly.

'You reckon?'

Something in her expression made Jennifer frown. 'He really got to you, didn't he?' she said slowly. 'I've never known you to lose your sense of humour like this before, and God knows we've had them all in here. What happened, did he make a pass at you when Melisande wasn't looking?'

'Why should he? You said yourself he'd got the lot; I can't think of a single reason why he should spare me a glance when he's got Melisande.'

'I can,' Jennifer replied. 'Several. For a start, you've got far more sex appeal. Oh, I know Melisande looks all soft and cuddly, but anyone can see she's as hard as nails underneath, while you . . . Are you sure he didn't make a pass?'

'Positive. Now, can we please change the subject?'

'Okay,' Jennifer agreed cheerfully. 'What do you want to talk about? Oh, help! I've just remembered, you-know-who rang. Said he'd pick you up at eight. I didn't know you had a date with him tonight.'

'I don't—at least not officially. He did say something about us having dinner together last week, but I've already told him I . . .'

'You don't date married men,' Jenneifer supplied with another grin. 'You certainly believe in making things difficult for yourself, don't you? With his influence . . .'

'I don't want his influence, Jen,' India cut in with unusual crispness. 'I like Mel, and I value his friendship. I've known him for over three years— ever since I first opened this salon. My accountant introduced him to me—in fact it was Mel who first told me about these premises . . .'

'Well, you could do worse, you know,' Jennifer pointed out judiciously. 'He's mad about you— anyone can see that.'

'He's married,' India replied stubbornly. 'And besides, I don't love him.'

'Love? Who needs it?' Jennifer demanded sourly. 'You know, for all that I'm three years younger than you, I sometimes feel old enough to be your mother.'

'If you were, you'd hardly be encouraging me to go out with someone else's husband,' India pointed out dryly, but Jennifer merely raised her eyebrows.

'You're kidding! With a man as wealthy as Mel, mothers tend to forget an unimportant thing like an existing wife.'

Was she being stupid? India wondered several hours later as she locked the salon and stepped out into the crisp evening air. It wasn't very far from the salon to where she lived. She had been lucky enough to be able to buy the top floor of one of an old row of Victorian terraced houses, just before they became fashionable, and she loved the privacy and space it gave her.

Mel had hinted on more than one occasion that he wanted to put their relationship on a more serious footing, but she had always reminded him of his wife.

Perhaps it was foolish at her age to virtually abandon the idea of a home, husband and children of her own simply because she had yet to meet the man who would be her ideal. It might have helped if she had known what she was looking for. All she did know was that as yet she had not met him; the man who would touch her emotions deeply enough for her to be able to break through the barriers of distrust erected during her vulnerable teens.

The phone rang just as she was unlocking her front door. She reached for it, dropping her coat and bag on the attractively re-covered Victorian chair which was the only piece of furniture in the tiny hall.

She had several good friends who often rang her, but she knew before she heard his voice who it would be on this occasion.

'You got my message?'

'Yes, I did, Mel, but I'm afraid . . .'

'Please come, I want to talk to you—seriously. Please, India, I need to talk to you. I'd suggest that you come round here to my place, but I know you'd refuse, and as I'm hardly likely to get an invitation to your retreat, dinner seemed to be the only alternative.'

Recognising the strain in his voice, India gave way.

'I'll pick you up—about eight. We're dining at Jardine's.'

It was one of the more exclusive new restaurants which had recently opened and tables were not easily come by, but then to a man of Mel Taylor's influence nothing would be impossible.

He had done very well for himself, India recognised, having built up an enviable business empire from one small company, and India suspected he was drawn to her because she too had had to struggle, and knew the value of what one earned by one's own achievements. About his home background she knew very little apart from the fact that he had a wife and two small children, both boys, who attended an exclusive prep school. Although it was never said India guessed that there was a tremendous gulf between father and sons in the way that there often was between a parent who had been forced to work hard, building up a fortune from very small beginnings, and the children who enjoyed the style of life that fortune could purchase. She had once heard it mentioned that Mel had married 'above himself'—an expression which she detested, and which she considered in Mel's case was grossly un-merited, as he was a man of extremely refined taste, gentle and kind, and she wondered if it was perhaps this which had given rise to his marital problems. They were not something she cared to discuss with him, and she had never pried into his private life, despite the length of time she had known him. In fact it was only quite recently that she had seen him on a regular basis, certainly within the last six months, and it had not been until a couple of months ago that she had realised that Mel was subtly trying to steer their relationship into more intimate waters.

As they were dining out she made herself a light snack, and ate it sitting on a stool in the tiny kitchen she had planned and designed herself. Her flat was reasonably spacious; a large lounge with tall classical windows, a small dining room which had looked cold and dark until she had cleverly redecorated it in shades of crimson offset by white; two bedrooms each with their own bathroom, and a small study.

Decorating and furnishing the flat had been a labour of love which India had thoroughly enjoyed. Her parents had had several good pieces of furniture inherited from older members of the family, and India had spent much of her spare time combing antique shops and street markets until she found what she was looking for. The street markets served two purposes. In addition to finding the odd piece of furniture she had been lucky enough to come across several pieces of old lace which she meticulously repaired herself and kept for her own designs.

Usually after her evening meal, when she was

relaxed, she found herself gravitating towards her
sketch pad, and sometimes the ideas which came to
her then proved far better than those she laboured
over in her work-room at the salon, but tonight there
would not be time for any work.

Jardine's attracted a sophisticated fashion-conscious crowd of diners, and India chose carefully
from her own surprisingly limited wardrobe. When
one was constantly making things for other people
there never seemed to be enough time to make for
oneself, and as India was the first to admit, she was
fussy about her clothes.

The outfit both Melisande and to some extent
Simon Herries had mocked earlier in the day was
one she had had for several years. The plain silk
blouse had been bought in Paris and she loved the
texture of the fabric and the neatly tailored lines of
the garment. It had cost a small fortune, but India
considered that she had more than had her money's
worth in terms of wear. The grey flannel skirt was
one of her own, beautifully styled and cut, top-stit-
ching emphasising the neat centre pleat, and with it
she often wore a slightly darker grey cashmere car-
digan with tiny pearl buttons. The flamboyant
clothes favoured by many of her clients simply were
not 'her'.

Sliding a soft black velvet dress with a high neck
edged with cream lace and three-quarter-length
sleeves off its hanger, she left it on the bed while she
had her bath.

Her bathroom possessed both a bath and a separate shower, and while in the mornings a quick
shower was all she had time for, whenever possible
she preferred a luxurious soak in scented water.

'Arpège' was her favourite perfume; she had read somewhere that women who favoured the aldehydic floral scents, such as Arpège, Chanel No. 5, and Madame Rochas, projected a cool, in-control image, and that they were in fact very much 'establishment' fragrances. Perhaps it had something to do with her childhood experiences; this desire to uphold traditions, and encourage permanence, India did not really know. What she did know, however, was that when she had tried to switch to a different type of scent, something more sensual and oriental, she had found it impossible to do so.

She dressed quickly and efficiently, a black silk camisole and matching slip trimmed lavishly with lace; sheer black stockings—one of the pleasures of being successful was that it was possible to indulge in such luxuries without feeling guilty. As she slid the fine silk over her legs she paused, remembering Simon Herries' comment, and the way he had looked at her. She had found that look disturbing. She shrugged mentally. What did he, or his opinions, matter to her? He was not the type of man she was ever likely to want to impress—too physically dominant; almost too male for her tastes. She, unlike Jennifer, did not think he would be a good lover; he was too much aware of himself, she felt, although she had to admit that the procession of women through his life read like a *Beautiful People's Who's Who*.

The black velvet dress fitted her perfectly, the colour of the lace almost exactly matching the creamy texture of her skin.

Because she knew Mel would like it, she applied more make-up than normal, concentrating on emphasising her eyes, which because of their size and deep clarity of colour tended to look almost impossibly emerald.

It was in Paris that she had learned the importance of proper skin care, and she knew she was fortunate in having the type of bone structure which would never really age.

Again because Mel liked it, she wore her hair in a soft chignon, twisting into it a row of pearls which had been last year's Christmas present to herself. She was just applying perfume to her throat and wrists when she heard the door, and gathering up the black velvet evening coat designed to be worn over her dress she hurried to open it.

Mel's eyes widened appreciatively when he saw her. He bent his head towards her, but she moved slightly so that it was her cheek and not her mouth that he kissed.

'You look wonderful,' he said simply. 'I wish we were spending the evening alone.'

His voice and eyes were heavy with pain, and India sensed that something was troubling him.

'Not now,' he forestalled her. 'We'll talk over dinner.'

He wasn't driving his own car, but had come in a taxi. It had rained since India had left the salon, and the streets glistened like liquorice, reflecting the brilliantly lit store windows.

Neither of them spoke, although to India the atmosphere felt heavy with sadness.

CHAPTER TWO

DOWN a narrow street not far from Hyde Park, Jardine's was in what had once been a small mews.

Wall-to-wall expensive cars lined the cul-de-sac; a doorman appeared from under a striped awning to open the taxi door, the requisite bay trees standing sentinel in their tubs either side of the door.

As they entered the restaurant India noticed at least half a dozen famous faces and repressed a small sigh. In many ways she would far rather have eaten in the cheerful family-run Italian restaurant round the corner from her flat, but she recognised that Mel probably thought he was giving her a special treat, which was merely another pointer against their relationship, she reflected. If he really knew and understood her, he would have known that she had little liking for the trappings of success.

She studied her reflection critically for a moment in the cloakroom while she waited for the girl to take her cloak. The black velvet dress accentuated the creamy pallor of her skin, her neck rising slenderly and elegantly above the crisp lace, her eyes deeply and intensely green, almost too large for the delicacy of her face. But India saw nothing of the delicate beauty of her features; all her concentration was focused on her dress. Most of the other female diners were wearing evening dresses of one sort or another, the majority of them baring vast expanses of flesh. Was she prudish? She shrugged the thought aside, but it was not quite as easy to dismiss the memory of the manner in which Simon Herries had commented on the contrast between her clothes and the sheer silk stockings she had been wearing with them; almost as though he had been accusing her of deliberately trying to project a false image of school-girlish innocence. Drat the man! What did it matter what he and his kind thought?

They were shown to a table discreetly set aside from the majority of the others in a small alcove, but which by its very 'apartness' negated its intimacy by making it almost a focal point of the room.

The restaurant had not been open for very long, and had been designed to represent a Victorian con-servatory, the marble-topped tables set among a profusion of indoor plants, cleverly illuminated in the evening.

With such a vast expanse of glass the restaurant could have been cold, but fortunately the owners had had the foresight to install an efficient central heating system.

'All we need is for a parrot to come flying down out of the foliage,' Mel commented jokingly to her as he studied the menu.

'Either that or Tarzan,' India agreed.

'Don't you like it? We could go somewhere else. This place is all the rage at the moment and I thought . . .'

'It's fine. Give me a quick nudge if you see me staring round open-mouthed—the last time I saw so many stars was on television, at a Royal Command Performance.'

'Umm, it does seem to be patronised rather

heavily by the acting profession. What do you fancy to eat?'

'I think I'll start with the seafood platter, and then perhaps chicken in white wine.'

Mel gave her order to the hovering waiter, adding his own. He was a very traditional male, India reflected; not a male chauvinist, but a man who genuinely believed that women were the frailer sex and needed protecting. He reminded her in many ways of her father; she felt comfortable and safe with him, or at least she had done until recently.

He waited until their food arrived and the wine had been poured before mentioning the reason for his invitation, for once his normal businesslike self-control deserting him.

'India, you know how I feel about you,' he blurted out without preamble. 'Oh, I know you refuse to take me seriously, but you aren't either a fool or insensitive, I know that. I also know how you feel about my marriage, and it's to your credit, although there have been times when I've wished that you were less . . . old-fashioned.'

'Old-fashioned?' India queried lightly.

'Moral,' Mel submitted, 'even though in my heart of hearts I wouldn't have you any other way. I only wish I'd met you ten years ago, before I married Alison. Even if you were willing to have an affair with me, I don't think I could. I don't think I've got it in me to destroy that shining look of self-respect you always seem to have about you. India . . . If I divorced Alison would you marry me?'

She had known it was coming, but nevertheless it was a shock. Her face went white, her hand trembling as she reached for her glass. Her fingers reached for the stem, her emotion making her clumsy, and as the glass overturned she stared helplessly at the wine flowing across the table and on to the floor.

Unfortunately she had barely touched it, and while a waiter discreetly mopped up, Mel tried to reassure her that it didn't matter.

'It happens all the time—and you didn't even break the glass,' he joked. 'Even if you had it isn't the end of the world!'

India herself didn't really know why she should be so distraught, unless it was because she was so rarely clumsy. Fortunately the wine had not gone on her dress, but her fingers were a little sticky, and it was as she bent down to open her handbag and find her handkerchief that she became aware of being watched. She raised her head slowly, disbelief mirrored in her eyes as she glanced across the restaurant and encountered the hard, inimical grey eyes of Simon Herries. Her heart started to thump uncomfortably, her mouth dry with a tension which owed nothing to the contretemps with the wine glass.

Melisande was with him, but as yet the actress seemed to be unaware of India's presence, and it was as though the two of them, India and Simon Herries, were locked in some primaeval conflict, which excluded the other diners as though they simply did not exist.

'India . . .'

'Oh . . . I'm sorry,' she muttered.

'You look as though you've seen a ghost.'

'I wish he was. Oh, I'm sorry,' she apologised, seeing Mel's worried frown. 'It's just Melisande's latest man. She brought him to the salon this afternoon, and for some reason he rubbed me up the wrong way, I don't know why.'

'Who is he?'

'Simon Herries—you must have heard of him. He's always appearing in the gossip columns . . . Are you all right?' she asked, noticing the sudden jerky movement he made, his face oddly pale. 'Mel . . .'

'I'm fine . . . It's nothing, India,' he began with a kind of desperation, 'Would you . . . would you marry me if I divorced Alison?'

She reached across the table, touching his hand with hers, her expression compassionate.

'I admire you, Mel; I value your friendship, and there's no one I would rather turn to in a crisis, but . . .'

'But you don't love me,' he supplied heavily. 'Well, I guess I knew what the answer was going to be, but a man can't help hoping.'

'I wish I could love you,' India surprised herself by saying. 'Sometimes I wonder if I'm capable of love—the kind of love which burns so fiercely that nothing else matters.'

There was understanding and pain in Mel's eyes as he looked at her.

'You are, my darling,' he told her huskily. 'It's just that as yet you haven't met the right man, but never doubt yourself in that way, and never demean yourself by giving yourself to someone without it.'

It was an oblique reference to the fact that she had never had a lover, and India was a little surprised by his astuteness. It was not a subject she had ever discussed with him—or indeed anyone, and she could only hope that no one else found her equally transparent. Knowing in what light the majority of her acquaintances would view a twenty-five-year-old virgin, she took immense pains at least outwardly to preserve a modern, almost cool attitude towards sex.

'Darling, you never told me you were dining here tonight.' Melisande's sharp eyes appraised Mel. 'You're looking tired, Mel,' she told him, adding to India, 'What have you been doing to him, darling?'

Simon Herries was at her side. It was apparent that they had finished their meal and were on the point of departure. Mel looked even paler than he had done before. He had stood up when Melisande approached the table, and although he was a tall man, Simon Herries topped him by several inches. Even she had to tilt her head to look up at him, India acknowledged; something that was quite rare when she wore, as she was doing tonight, in defiance of smaller girl friends' advice, high-heeled shoes.

'We're going on to Tokyo Joe's,' Melisande told them, mentioning one of the newer clubs. 'Why don't you come with us? I've read this divine new play; the lead part could have been written for me . . . but it costs a fortune to put on a production now-adays . . .'

She was looking at Mel as she spoke, but he didn't respond, and the actress pouted a little.

'Persuade them to come with us, darling,' she demanded of Simon Herries. 'It will be fun.'

'I suspect the sort of "fun" Melford and Miss Lawson have in mind requires only two partici-pants,' he drawled in response, 'despite the almost puritanical appearance of Miss Lawson.'

'Darling!' Melisande protested in half shocked, half fascinated breathy tones, her eyes rounding with surprise. Mel was already on his feet, and India saw the way his fingers bunched into his palm, the giveaway muscle beating sporadically in his clenched jaw.

She reached towards him instinctively, her voice low as she begged him to let matters alone.

'Such modesty; such quiet, well-bred manners!' Simon Herries mocked savagely. 'No one looking at you would guess that what you're really doing is stealing someone else's husband, or is it simply that you've discovered that it turns some men—especially older men—on to project that quakerish, "touch-me not" image?'

He turned on his heel before India could respond, his hand under Melisande's elbow as he escorted her out of the restaurant. None of the other diners seemed to have noticed the small piece of byplay. India looked at Mel. He was as white as a ghost, the skin stretched ageingly over his bones, his eyes pained and defeated.

'He had no right to speak to you like that,' he said thickly. 'No right at all. God, I could have killed him!'

'Forget it. It doesn't matter,' India lied lightly.

'I hadn't realised what I was doing to you, what interpretation others would put upon our friendship.' His mouth twisted bitterly. 'And all for nothing! India, there's something I have to tell you. Oh, if I thought there was the slightest chance that you might marry me . . . Alison, my wife, is pregnant . . .' He grimaced when he saw India's expression. 'Yes, I know, but then, my darling, men *are* like that. Despite what I feel for you I still make love to my wife. Despicable, aren't I? And knowing you as I do, I haven't told you before, because I knew you would never let me leave her while she was carrying my child. But that isn't all of it. After the boys Alison was told she wasn't to have any more children. Perhaps that's why . . .' he frowned. 'God, I shouldn't be burdening you with all this, but the fact of the matter is that after Johnny was born we took to sleeping separately. She had a bad time, and then the doctor warned us that she wasn't to have any more. The pill didn't agree with her . . . and what with one thing or another we just never got it together again. Until now. Her parents came to spend a weekend with us along with her brother and his wife. We needed the extra bedroom space, so I spent the night with her . . .'

'What will she do?' India asked, her mouth dry. 'Have an abortion?'

Mel shook his head. 'No, she's totally against the idea, and I have to confess that so am I. No, tonight was the final tie-breaker. If you'd agreed to marry me, I would have asked Alison for a divorce. I'm fortunate enough to be able to support two wives, two families, but as you won't, I feel I owe to my son, or daughter, whichever the case may be, to at least make an effort to provide a stable home. Alison isn't well, and . . .'

'Does she . . . does she know how you feel, I mean . . .'

'About you?' Mel shook his head. 'Not specifically. 'Oh, she knows that all is not as it should be, perhaps even how I feel about you, but nothing else. I'm going to go away for a while, India. I know that my duty, I suppose I should call it, lies with Alison and my children, but I need time to come to terms with it, time to gather my strength, if you like . . .'

'Where will you go?'

'I haven't decided.'

They left the restaurant in a silence which continued during the taxi journey, almost morose on Mel's part, and pitying on India's—not just for Mel, but for his wife as well, and it wasn't until the taxi stopped that she realised where they were. The taxi had come to a standstill outside the expensive block of apartments where Mel lived.

'Come in and have a drink with me, please,' he begged, and India hadn't the heart to refuse.

She had been in his apartment before, but never late at night, alone with him. It had a curiously sterile appearance, despite the obvious expense of the furniture and fittings.

'Alison hates this place,' he told India over their drink. 'She prefers the country. I think I'll give the apartment up. After all, I've got to a position in life now, where I can quite easily work from home ... Alison and I should never have married. We're too different.'

'How did you meet?' India asked him gently, sensing his need to talk.

'At a charity function. She was what was then called a deb—her mother's family are very well connected; not much money but generations of blueblood and the "right" marriages. She was small, and dark, and was the only person there who didn't seem to look down on me. I was very conscious in those days of my "nouveau-richeness". To cut a long story short, we both convinced ourselves that what we felt for one another was love and we got married. It didn't take very long for the gilt to tarnish. Alison tried to re-model me along the lines of her friends' husbands; and then the boys came along and she seemed to lose interest in me altogether . . .'

'You loved her once,' India reminded him softly, 'and she loved you. You both have a responsibility to your children and to each other.'

'Responsibility!' Mel laughed bitterly. 'God, that's a sterile, relentless word. Come on, I'd better get you a taxi.'

'It isn't very far—I'll walk.'

'No way.'

Reluctantly she allowed him to order her a taxi, smiling a little at his insistence on accompanying her downstairs to the street when it arrived.

'What do you think's going to happen to me?' she teased, her expression changing when she saw the haunted look in his eyes. Oblivious of the taxi and the passing traffic, she put her hands on either side of his face.

'Oh, Mel, please don't look like that,' she whispered. 'It will all work out . . . I know it will.'

'Will it?' With a muffled groan he pulled her into his arms, kissing her with a fierce urgency which she did nothing to prevent, knowing in her heart that this was his final goodbye.

Held fast in his arms, overwhelmed by pity, she was unaware of the sleek green Ferrari speeding past them, or of the bitter cynicism in the eyes of the man who observed them.

Another hour and she'd have to call it day, India decided wearily. She had spent the last week working on designs for dresses for one of her oldest customers and her daughter for the latter's eighteenth birthday party. Celia Harvey was small and plump with smooth dark hair and an almost Madonna-like expression, and India would dearly like to have dressed her in something soft and flowing, almost pre-Raphaelite, but she had been told in no uncertain terms by the young lady in question that she wanted something slinky and sexy à la Anthony Price. Her mother had raised her eyebrows in despair, and India sympathised.

Well, either Celia would like it, or she would have to find herself another designer, she decided at length, frowning critically over the multitude of careful drawings she had sketched. Her head was beginning to ache with familiar tension and she flexed her back, rubbing the base of her neck tiredly. Jennifer and the girls from the workroom had left hours before, and outside the streets were in darkness. She glanced at her watch. Nearly nine. Another evening almost gone, and all she wanted to do was to go home, soak in a hot bath and then go to bed.

She grimaced as she remembered the letter she had received that morning from her accountant. It was time they had a meeting, he reminded her. The trouble was that her clientele was expanding all the time, and it was becoming too much of a burden for her to design, and run the financial side of her business. The obvious answer was to take on someone to deal with the financial side, but who? It was at times like this that she missed Mel—selfishly, she admitted. She hadn't seen him since the evening they had dined together at Jardine's, and she had presumed that he had gone away, as he had said he intended to do, to sort himself out.

She herself was badly in need of a holiday. Summer had never seemed farther away. London was having one of the worst springs on record, with cold, blustery winds, and almost constant rain.

Of course it was impossible to find a taxi when she emerged into the street. Rather than wait for a bus she set off at a brisk pace in the direction of her flat, and got caught between bus stops in an icy downpour which soaked through her raincoat, the fierce wind making it impossible to keep her umbrella up. To cap it all, a speeding car, screeching round a corner in front of her, sent freezing cold water all over her legs, soaking through the hem of her coat, and by the time she reached the sanctuary of her flat she was both frozen and bad-tempered.

She ran a bath, and luxuriated in it for half an hour, feeling the strain of the day seeping away. With her newly shampooed hair wrapped in a towel she padded into her small kitchen to heat a bowl of soup. When she worked as she was doing at the moment her appetite seemed to desert her. She could have done without Celia's dress right now; she already had enough orders to keep her going until the autumn.

She was becoming obsessed with the salon, she told herself wryly. Jenny had been saying only that morning that she never went out anywhere any longer. She had pleaded the excuse of there simply being not enough time, but Jenny had scoffed and quoted direfully, 'All work and no play make's a spinster dull and grey.'

Something must have happened to her sense of humour lately, India acknowledged, because the comment had jared.

'Don't worry about it,' Jenny had said later when she apologised. 'We all suffer from it from time to time.'

When she had unwisely asked, 'Suffer from what?' Jenny had eyed her assessingly and said, 'Frustration, of course.'

Was that the answer? She wasn't consciously aware of the need for a lover, but then perhaps she had grown so used to ignoring her natural urges that she was no longer attuned to them; and spring was notorious for having an odd effect on the lonely.

But she wasn't lonely, she told herself. She had plenty of . . .

The phone rang, cutting across her thoughts. She padded into the hall and lifted the receiver,

'Miss Lawson?' a crisp male voice intoned decisively. 'You may not remember me. Simon Herries.'

Her free hand clutched at the silk robe she had pulled on as though by some means he was able to see how little she was wearing. Her mouth had gone dry, her heart pounding heavily.

'Yes, Mr Herries,' she managed. 'What can I do for you?'

'It's not what you can do for me, but what you can do for Melisande,' she heard him say in response.

'Melisande?' India frowned. 'I thought she was in the States filming.'

'Yes, she is, but she's due back this weekend. I'm organising a welcome home party for her at her apartment and she particularly wanted me to invite you.'

'Me? But . . .'

'I hope you can make it. Several colleagues of mine from South-Mid Television will be there, and

Melisande tells me that you're quite keen to break into television designing.'

'Not particularly.'

What on earth was it about this man that set her teeth on edge; brought the tiny hairs on her skin up in atavistic dislike?

'Melisande will be very disappointed . . .'

'I don't honestly know if I can make it,' India temporised. 'I have rather a lot of work on at the moment . . . I'll have to look in my diary.'

'Very well. I'll ring you at the salon tomorrow and check if you can make it,' he told her coolly.

After he had rung off India found it impossible to settle. She wandered about the flat, touching things, fidgeting, full of a nervous energy which eventually drove her into her small study where she worked until at last tiredness began to claim her.

She told Jenny about the invitation over coffee the following morning.

'You're going, of course,' her secretary exclaimed. 'You lucky thing!'

'Well . . .' India demurred, 'I don't know if I can manage it, we've so much on at the moment.'

'Nothing that can't wait,' Jenny told her briskly. 'Look, I've got all the schedules here. You can't work all day, half the night and all weekend as well!'

'There's Celia's dress . . .'

'Blow Celia! I don't know why you're wasting so much time on her anyway. If she wants to dress herself up like a plump shiny Christmas tree let her. Seriously, you ought to go. You're the boss, I know, but I like my job and I feel I've got to do all I can to protect it, which includes making sure my boss doesn't kill herself through overwork. One party; half a dozen hours out of your life . . .'

Put like that it did make her reluctance seem a little foolish, India was forced to admit. And why was she so reluctant? She didn't know; she only knew that it had something to do with Simon Herries. Something; didn't she mean everything?

'You know,' Jenny exclaimed judiciously, when they had finished their coffee, 'I think you're scared to go. Are you, India?'

'No . . . No, of course not. Why should I be?' Why indeed?

The phone rang as she finished speaking.

'It's Simon Herries,' Jenny, who had taken the call, announced to her in a whisper. 'Shall I tell him you're going?'

'I'll tell him myself, thanks very much,' India replied dryly, taking the proffered receiver.

'Are you able to make it?' he asked without preamble, obviously not seeing any need to waste time in unnecessary conversation.

Conscious of Jenny in the room, India forced herself to sound calm and relaxed.

'Yes . . . yes, I think so.'

'Good. Melisande would have been disappointed if you couldn't. She particularly wanted you to come. So did I.'

Why should her pulses race simply because of those three casually spoken words?

'Oh, by the way, I nearly forgot. Don't bother with a taxi, I'll pick you up. Eight, at your flat—I know the address.'

He had hung up before India could say a word.

'Well,' Jenny demanded, 'are you going?'

'It looks like it.'

'Great. Now all you have to do is to decide what to wear.'

CHAPTER THREE

FAMOUS last words, India thought ruefully, three days later, surveying the contents of her wardrobe. Knowing Melisande, the majority of the other guests would be culled from the ranks of the beautiful and/ or socially prominent; people with whom she could scarcely compete.

Positive thinking, India told herself. She might not be either wealthy or titled, but she was young, reasonably attractive, and if she wasn't dressed at least as eye-catchingly as the other female guests she had no one to blame but herself.

However, that was half the trouble. Her own personal preference for plain, unfussy clothes revealed itself in the garments hanging in her cupboard. If she knew Melisande and the rest of her crowd, the women would be dressed in the very latest fashions, the more outré and daring the better. She would look like a minnow in the midst of a whole host of brightly painted tropical fish!

She fingered her velvet dress, frowning as she pictured Simon Herries, looking over it—and her— with that cynical knowingness that so infuriated her. Without giving herself time to change her mind she rang for a taxi.

When it came she was ready, having bathed and carefully applied her make-up while she waited.

She gave him directions and asked him to wait while she slipped into the salon.

It didn't take her long to find what she was looking for—a dress she had designed for one of her clients to wear over Christmas. Unfortunately the girl had broken her leg the week before the dance and the dress had remained unworn.

Grabbing it off the rail, together with its protective wrapping, India hurried back to the waiting taxi.

'Sorry about that,' she apologised to the waiting driver, 'but I needed to collect something.'

'Don't worry about it, love,' she was assured as the taxi driver glanced down at the dress she was carrying over her arm, grinning at her as he opened the taxi door.

'At least you'll never be able to use the same excuse as my missus; not with a whole shopful of things to choose from—always complaining that she ain't got anything to wear she is.'

India glanced at her watch as she stepped out of the taxi in front of her flat.

Fifteen minutes before Simon Herries was due to pick her up. With a bit of luck she should just about be ready. She had no desire to be forced into asking him into the flat while she finished dressing.

India was choosy about who she invited into her home. The salon was where she saw most of her clients—either there or at their homes; and she treasured the privacy and solitude of the flat which she kept firmly separate from the salon.

Most of the decorating she had done herself, unlike the salon; and she had chosen furniture and furnishings which appealed to her.

That, she reflected, unlocking the door, was one

of the pleasures of accounting to no one but oneself. There was no one to question one's taste!

The kitchen, with its mellow wooden units and tiled worktops, reflected her love of natural products as opposed to synthetics. The honey-coloured tiles on the worktops and the floor had been bought on a business trip to Spain, and their warm colour always reminded her of the brilliant sunshine and warmth of Spain. The kitchen had pretty green and white curtains made up in a French fabric she had found in Liberty's; a comfortable basket chair possessed cushions of the same fabric, and green plants in pretty pots added a touch of extra colour and freshness.

The comfortable lounge was furnished with an assortment of items India had purchased over the years; an old bookcase which she had had stripped and cleaned; a huge settee which she had bought in a sale and subsequently re-covered in cream; and most prized of all, probably, the traditional Persian rug which she had bought with the profit from her first year in business on her own account.

In her bedroom, which reflected her taste for fresh, natural colours, India stripped off the clothes she had worn to go to the salon and unzipped the protective cover from the dress she had brought from there.

Made of crinkly gold tissue, the strapless bodice moulded the firm thrust of her breasts, emphasising the slenderness of her waist and clinging seductively to the feminine curve of her hips and the slender length of her legs.

The dress needed no adornment, and the only

jewellery India wore was a thick twisted rope of gold hugging her throat.

She did not possess any gold sandals, but had an elegant pair of black suede evening shoes which she had bought in Paris, and which were so high that they mde her tower above most of the men she knew; perhaps it was a power complex, she thought wryly, this refusal to acknowledge male pride and resort, as so many of her tall sisters did, to wearing flat or low-heeled shoes.

Over the dress she intended to wear her black velvet evening cloak, and she was just reaching for it when she heard the doorbell ring. Smothering the butterflies swarming in her stomach, she checked her appearance in the mirror, a little taken aback by the reflection staring at her.

For some reason the gold fabric seemed to inten-sify the dark richness of her hair and the creamy perfection of her skin. Although she was very slim, her breasts were marginally fuller than the girl's for whom the gown had originally been designed, and the strapless bodice seemed to draw provocative at-tention to their firm upthrust.

It was too late to change now, she told herself, reaching for her cloak and evening bag, and switch-ing off the bedroom light.

In the lounge she left a table light burning, a soli-tary pool of colour reflecting downwards from the cream shade on to the richness of her prized rug.

She opened the door, composing her features into her 'professional' mask.

Her first thought was that Simon Herries seemed larger than she remembered; then she realised that the proximity of her small hall meant that she was far closer to him, and actually forced to look up at him as he stepped inside.

That made India frown. She had been on the point of stepping out of the flat as he moved forward and the two paces were enough to bring them close enough for her to be able to smell the fresh, sharp scent of his aftershave. It enveloped her in a spicy, entirely masculine scent, and she wondered briefly if he was equally as aware of her Arpège, a thought which she quickly dismissed as unimportant and stupid.

'Do you think it's wise to leave that on?' He was looking over India's shoulder, into the lounge where she had left the lamp burning, and beneath her make-up India felt her face colour with mingled resentment and anger. Another step and he would be inside the lounge; penetrating her private sanctuary, violating her privacy. She moved instinctively, impeding his progress, her voice curt and clipped as she said coolly,

'I always leave it on.'

'Why? To deter thieves? Because you're frightened of the dark?'

His eyes swung from her collection of attractive, but with the exception of her rug, relatively inexpensive furniture, to her cool, remote face, and he drawled mockingly, 'Hardly. So why . . .?'

'Perhaps because it's welcoming to come home to.'

'Ah, yes!' Something gleamed in his eyes; something alien and almost frightening. 'Of course,' he said softly, 'you would know all about the . . . benefits of being welcoming.'

If there was a double meaning to the words, it escaped India.

'Has it ever occurred to you that it might not be safe?'

Before she could stop him, Simon Herries had walked past her to the lamp, swiftly switching it off, but not, she noticed, before those all-seeing dark grey eyes had glanced swiftly and assessingly over the room and its contents.

'Very nice,' he commented as they left. 'You're a very fortunate young woman, India Lawson. Your own business—a successful business at that—youth; looks.' They were out on the street and beneath lashes far darker and thicker than any mere man had a right to possess his eyes assessed her contours cloaked in the black velvet.

What was she supposed to do, India fumed; fawn ingratiatingly? But Simon Herries hadn't finished.

'A devoted admirer . . . even if he is someone else's husband . . . He must be very fond of you to have set you up with the salon. Prime site in Mayfair—it can't have come cheap.'

They were standing on the kerb in front of the immaculate Ferrari, Simon Herries had reached towards the passenger door and was opening it for India to get in, but she stood her ground, sparks kindling in her eyes,

'For your information, no one "set me up with the salon", as you put it. All I have has been achieved through my own hard work!'

'And Melford Taylor hasn't helped you in the slightest, is that what you're trying to say?' He was sneering outright now, and for two pins India would have walked off and left him standing, but two things stopped her. One was her own pride; if she ran now it was tantamount to admitting that his accusations had some basis; and the other was that she could not run anywhere, because Simon Herries' lean, hard fingers were gripping her wrist like a manacle; his superior weight forcing her into the passenger seat of the car. Her wrist was released and the door was closed. India rubbed it covertly, staring stonily out of the passenger window as she felt the cold rush of air as the driver's door opened and she felt the car depress as Simon Herries slid alongside her.

'Sulking?' he commented ten minutes later when India was still staring furiously ahead of her. 'It won't alter the truth.'

'The truth!' India turned to face him, her mouth taut with anger. 'I doubt if a man like you could recognise it!'

'Men like me are the only ones who do recognise it,' came the pithy reply, 'simply because they've had so much experience of the opposite sex. Your sex never cease to amaze me with their ability to contort "truth" to suite their own requirements; their own careers. Believe me, I know.'

'I'm sure you do!'

In the darkness of the car India could feel him staring at her, her eyes drawn involuntarily to his hands on the wheel, holding it with cool easy confidence; the way he would hold a woman, and she shivered with some prescient knowledge she could scarcely comprehend. What on earth was the matter with her?

The traffic was thinning out. India glanced at the dashboard clock, amazed to see that they had been travelling for well over half an hour. She frowned, searching the dark for a familiar landscape, and demanded abruptly, 'Is it far?'

'Is what far?' came the cool reply.

Fear gnawed edgily at India's already over-stretched nerves.

'Don't play games with me!' she snapped. 'You know perfectly well what I mean. Is it far to Melisande's flat?'

'Not particularly.'

No further information was forthcoming, and India was forced to contain her growing anger in a fuming silence; either that or be drawn into further bickering. Abominable man! she thought crossly. She could almost believe that he had been deliberately trying to goad her into losing her temper. She shot him a suspicious glance, watching the dark lashes flick downwards in answer to her scrutiny, although he never lifted his eyes from the road.

The Ferrari was picking up speed. India had fastened her seat-belt when she got in, and that, combined with the luxury of the deep leather seats, combined to hold her snugly in place, even when the car veered abruptly to the right. She just had time to see the road sign before suburban darkness swallowed them up again, and what she read on it had her turning ashen-faced to the man seated next to her.

'This isn't the way to Melisande's! It said on that signpost, M4, Bath and South Wales.'

'So it did,' Simon Herries agreed smoothly.

'Well, aren't you going to turn back?'

'Why?'

'Why?' India stared at him in disbelieving silence. 'Because we're going the wrong way, that's why!'

'Oh no, we're not.' The words were spoken so

softly that at first she couldn't believe she had actually heard them, but as though to reinforce them, Simon Herries continued expressionlessly, 'We're going exactly the way I planned we would go when I asked you to come to Melisande's party.' His mouth curled sardonically. 'I knew you'd find the bait irresistible.'

'Bait?' India said tonelessly. She was beyond feeling; beyond anything, apart from trying to come to terms with what was happening to her.

'Yes, the lure of a possible TV designing contract. That was why you agreed to come, of course.' For a moment India was too stupefied to speak, and then all at once she found her voice, questions tumbling over one another.

'What is this? Where's Melisande? Where are you taking me?'

'Which shall I answer first?' he mused sardonically. 'This, my dear India, is a form of—shall I call it retribution? A theatrical word to use, perhaps; justice is more how I think of it. As to Melisande,' he continued, before India could question his first statement, 'to the best of my knowledge at this very moment she's in California. Now as to your third question, which was, I believe, "Where are you taking me?" he mimicked her own half furious, half fearful tones to perfection, much to India's chagrin, 'I'm taking you to a cottage I own in Dorset, where you and I shall spend the weekend together, returning to London on Monday morning, when I shall deposit you at your salon, having very publicly escorted you inside.

'Tomorrow morning I shall ring your efficient secretary from the cottage, and explain to her that

you'll be late for work on Monday, and why . . .'
His eyes gleamed in the darkness and it seemed to
India, completely unable to believe what she was
hearing, that there was Satanic madness in that dark
grey gleam.

'Being the inestimable character that she is,
she will naturally leap to the most appropriate
conclusions, and before the week is out, my dear
India, it should even have reached the ears of
that doting boy-friend of yours that you and I
have, to put it colloquially, become "very good
friends".'

'But why? I don't understand! You don't like me.
You don't . . .'

'Desire you?' He was mocking her openly, but
beneath the mockery India sensed a dangerous anger
held in check. 'No, I don't desire you.'

'Then why?' India demanded helplessly, running
through in her mind all the possible explanations for
his totally irrational behaviour. Could it be an elab-
orate joke? She glanced doubtfully at the iron cast of
his profile, the hard jaw, and set mouth.

'Try Melford Taylor,' the hatefully controlled
voice drawled above her ear, 'or better still, try
Melford's unfortunate wife—my cousin. Oh yes,' he
agreed when she turned dismayed eyes towards him,
'Alison is most definitely my cousin. Her parents
were the only stable family I knew after my own
divorced; they practically brought me up. Alison was
like a sister to me—in fact I was the one to introduce
her to Melford. I'm even godfather to his two sons.
You did know about them: about the fact that your
lover had children by another woman—his wife?' he
demanded with a savagery that found India totally

unprepared after the controlled calm of his earlier statements.

'And yet you felt no compunction about taking him away from those children, that wife.'

'But there's nothing! No one . . .'

'No one knows? Is that what you were going to say? Are you honestly such an insensitive fool that you don't think a woman who's lived with a man for ten years knows when her husband is involved with another woman? But you don't hold all the cards, you know. Alison is having another child; Melford's child . . .'

'I know.'

The quietness of the two words seemed to silence him for a moment. They were speeding down the M4 now, the Ferrari eating up the black miles, India's insides churning viciously as she tried to come to terms with what was happening to her.

'You know, but you still think he'll leave Alison and his family; divorce her so that he can marry you.'

'I don't want him to divorce her,' said India with perfect truth.

'No, you wouldn't, would you?' Simon Herries sneered. 'You'd much rather keep him dangling, blowing hot and cold, but you must have given him some encouragement. Alison told me not a month ago that she feared that Mel was on the point of leaving her.'

A month ago; just before he had heard Melisande saying that she was Mel's girl-friend. She turned to him, the impulsive words dying on her lips as she saw his expression. It would take more determination than she possessed to convince him of the truth. Well, let him think what he liked, she decided on a sudden spurt of wrath. Let him!

'So why have you kidnapped me?' she demanded. 'To drag me in front of Mel's wife and force me to give him up?'

'Alison has already endured enough humiliation. She's ten years older than you, and struggling with a difficult pregnancy—can you imagine what it would do to her to be confronted by you, her husband's bedfellow!'

His fingers curled round India's hand as she lifted the palm towards his face.

'On no, you don't, you vicious little hellcat!' he snarled suddenly.

'I'll tell Mel what you've done!' India threw at him, frighteningly close to tears.

'You won't have to,' came the soft threat. 'I imagine he'll know all about it all too soon—as far as you're concerned, that is. Why do you think I've gone to all this trouble? Not to see if you're as good in bed as Mel obviously believes, you can depend on that!'

'You wouldn't get the chance!' India hissed at him, too furious to bother denying his comments. 'You're the last man I'd share a bed, or anything else with!'

'Good. Keep on thinking like that and the weekend should go reasonably well. By the way, you'll enjoy the little twist I've added to our masquerade, I'm sure. Alison knows I'm coming down for the weekend, and she'll probably call round to see me. I'd like to see Mel's face when she tells him, all unknowingly, just who was spending the weekend with me, wouldn't you?'

'You . . . you sadist!' India spat out at him, reaching instinctively for the door handle. Heaven only knows what she would have done had it given beneath her furious fingers, she reflected seconds later, visualising her torn and broken body lying on the motorway, but it seemed that Simon Herries had anticipated her, and the door was well and truly locked.

'Oh no,' he said quietly. 'Until this weekend's over I'm not letting you out of my sight.'

'Whatever you do won't make any difference to Mel,' India told him. 'All I have to do is to tell him the truth.'

'The truth being that you spent the weekend with me,' he reminded her brutally. 'Mel is a man, India, once he knows that the rest will merely be extraneous; he'll believe that I'll have done what he quite naturally would have done in the same circumstances. Even were I to tell him that the weekend was quite platonic he wouldn't believe me. Such is the power of jealousy.'

'You're despicable . . . vile!' India hurled at him. 'You. . .'

'No more "despicable" or "vile" than you,' Simon replied hardily. 'Or don't you consider breaking up a marriage, a family, to be important? Couldn't you simply have been content with Mel's influence and money?'

'I've told you before, whatever I have I've worked for . . .'

She broke off as Simon threw back his head and laughed mirthlessly. 'Oh yes, I'm damn sure you have; does Mel know that you consider allowing him to make love to you "work", I wonder?' he sneered.

'Perhaps I ought to mention that in passing, adding of course that you found sleeping with me infinitely preferable. I've shocked you? Why, I wonder? Women like you don't merit the courtesy of silence, my dear; I would have thought you would have learned that before now.'

They turned off the motorway into a deserted A-road, which seemed to wind tortuously through unlit countryside, India growing more panicky with every passing minute. She had already abandoned any hope of convincing her captor that she was innocent of all the crimes of which he accused her, and her only hope of escape seemed to lie in persuading him to set her free on the proviso that she told Mel that she would have nothing further to do with him (an easy task, as this was what she had already done), but when she suggested it, the same mirthless laughter as before filled the car.

'You must be joking! I wouldn't trust you as far as I could throw you.'

'And if I were to tell you that you've got everything wrong; that I'm not Mel's lover, that I have no intention of breaking up his marriage—far from it . . .'

'Too late, my dear,' he responded dryly, negotiating a sharp bend. 'As I've already told you, I've learned to tell when a woman is telling the truth. Here we are,' he added as they reached the end of a narrow country road. 'Mrs Bridges from the village will have stocked the cottage for us. I told her I was bringing a friend with me, so we won't be interrupted. What's the matter?' he jeered, looking at her white face. 'Wishing it was Mel at your side?'

She would try and snatch the car keys as he got

out, India thought sickly, or failing that she would make a run for it . . .

The car stopped, the headlights illuminating what India would normally have considered a charming country house. Built of stone, with a deep bay window either side of an attractive open porch, it had a homely welcoming air which at other times would have drawn her irresistibly. She waited for Simon to get out of the car, but to her dismay he put it in gear and moved forward slowly. The garage door lifted and they slid inside, the door closing firmly behind them.

They were in a large garage with a courtesy door into the house; so much for her plans for escape, India thought bitterly, forced to wait until Simon uncoiled himself from the car and moved to her door to unlock it for her.

His hand on her elbow helped her out, changing to the grip of a gaoler as he escorted her towards the door. It hadn't been locked, but India noticed that he locked it after him, reaching up to switch on the lights.

They were in a laundry room, fitted with washing machine and freezer. Simon moved forward, forcing India to accompany him, as he opened the door to what was obviously the kitchen. It was generously proportioned and comfortable, with units similar to the ones in India's apartment, but these, she could tell, were craftsman-built, the wood smooth and rich. This was a family kitchen, she thought, staring round it; not that of a single, sophisticated man. In this kitchen she could imagine a toddler playing with a puppy while a baby slept in its cradle and their mother busied herself with the baking.

'What's the matter?' Simon jeered sardonically,

'Trying to put a price on it? You couldn't. I bought this as a tumbledown cottage with my first earnings . . .'

'And have spent a considerable amount on it since,' India retorted.

'In time and hard craft, yes—but money no. What's the matter? Are you surprised that I should find enjoyment in rebuilding and refashioning the past? But then you don't know me, do you?'

'And you don't know me!' India flung at him fiercely. 'You accuse me of trying to steal your cousin's husband, of breaking up their marriage, of . . .'

'Okay, that's enough. If you're going to have hysterics have them by the sink. That way it will be easier to throw cold water on them.'

Something about the hard, inimical gleam in his eyes made India realise that he wasn't joking.

'Come with me,' he commanded, grasping her arm firmly. She would be bruised in the morning; already her wrist was aching from the pressure of those merciless fingers.

'How can you be so sure of keeping me here all weekend?' India demanded as he marched her out into an attractive square hall, complete with grandfather clock which ticked melodiously, a Persian rug similar to her own a splash of rich colour against the stained and polished floorboards.

'Quite simple. Unless I'm with you, I intend to lock you in your room.' He produced a key from his pocket and held it up in front of her. 'One of the things the people who built in the nineteenth century insisted upon—privacy. All the doors in this house have locks; all the locks have keys, and guess who has all the keys? And forget any schoolgirl heroics such as clambering out of the window. I'm putting you in what was the nursery—another golden Victorian idea; they put bars across their nursery windows, in case you've forgotten.'

'I'm only surprised that you aren't forcing me to share *your* room!' India flung at him.

'What for?' Simon Herries asked her brutally. 'I'm not so frustrated that I need to avail myself of Mel's leavings; nor ever likely to be.'

This time India did slap him—hard, with the flat of her palm, the blow stinging her as much as it stung him, leaving her standing staring at the bright red mark of her hand against the taut flesh of his skin in sick horror. Even as a child she had had a dread of physical violence, had been a helpless target for bullies and had physically felt sick at the thought of being smacked. All her life she had considered that descending to physical violence represented the depths of human degradation, and yet now, in one split second, the emotions she had always kept so carefully leashed had boiled up inside her and forced her into a physical reaction which filled her with shame and self-loathing.

'Bitch!' Simon was breathing heavily, a muscle twitching spasmodically in his jaw. India watched it in horrified fascination.

'Oh no,' he said softly, as though he had read her mind, 'I'm not falling for that one. First provoke, then seduce? I'm too experienced a hand at the game to be taken in like that. What were you hoping to achieve? Surely you aren't optimistic or stupid enough to think you can change my mind? Or was it plain ordinary frustration? Mel has been away for quite a while, hasn't he? With a protector like him I expect it's worth your while not to take the risk of taking another lover when he's away. You're full of cute little touches like that, aren't you? Like leaving that lamp glowing so invitingly, for one . . . .'

'I hate you!' India choked out. 'I don't know how, but I'm going to make you pay for this—and pay dearly!'

He ignored her, half dragging her behind him as he mounted polished stairs, worn with the tread of many feet, to a small galleried landing. He fitted the key he had shown her into one of the doors, flinging it open and motioning her inside.

It was a small room, furnished with a bed and very little more. There was a basin in one corner, curtains hanging up at the window, and India, her imagination already working overtime, felt as though the room were enclosing her like a prison.

'Sorry about the lack of feminine frills,' Simon Herries told her in a tone that conveyed that he could not have cared less. 'If you want to use the bathroom, you've got fifteen minutes. It doesn't lock from the inside.'

His mouth thinned as India shot him a look of undiluted dislike.

'Oh, come on,' he demanded harshly, 'don't try that one on, we both know you're no shrinking virgin!'

'I haven't got anything to sleep in,' India protested, saying the first thing that came into her head, then blushing from head to foot as Simon Herries examined her slowly and thoroughly.

'No,' he agreed, 'if you're not used to sleeping alone you'll probably find it cold. It wouldn't do you any harm to suffer, but the last thing I want is to have a case of pneumonia on my hands. I'll see what I can find. Come with me.'

She was forced to follow him along the landing into another room which was plainly his own bedroom, furnished in dark blues, cream and rust, a masculine and very relaxing room.

'Wait here.' She was thrust down into the softness of the double bed while Simon Herries pulled open a drawer and removed a pair of silk pyjamas.

'No need to look like that,' he said dryly as she stared at them. 'They won't contaminate you. They've never been worn. I keep them for . . . appearances. Personally I don't like anything to come between me and . . . Blushing? Clever girl!' he drawled mock-admiringly. 'Mel must like that; he's an old-fashioned type at heart, which is probably why you've managed to get so much out of him. He never could resist a hard-luck story.'

'Unlike you. You're inhuman, do you know that?'

'You've got fifteen minutes if you want to use the bathroom,' he reminded her, and India was forced to concede that for the moment he held the upper hand and there was no way that she was going to be allowed to escape. Wearily she walked towards the bathroom, gripping the cream silk pyjamas.

Fourteen minutes later she emerged to find Simon Herries propped up against the wall. He surveyed her shiny make-up-free face and pyjama-clad figure coolly, his eyes dwelling for disturbing seconds on the thrust of India's breasts against the soft silk. She had thrown her cloak around her shoulders and she huddled into it instinctively as he looked at her, hating him for making her feel so aware of her own body, and hating herself for her reaction to his arrogant scrutiny.

The tiny bedroom was cold and cheerless. Sleep eluded her as she plotted and re-plotted on how she was going to get away. How she would love to be able to confront him with the truth—that all his careful planning had been for nothing. Poor Alison, she thought soberly; she felt sorry for Mel's wife, and thanked God that her conscience was clear. She heard water running in the bathroom and tensed instinctively, her mouth dry and her heart thudding. What was the matter with her? She had nothing to fear physically from Simon Herries, he had made that more than clear. All she had to do was to wait; sooner or later she would get an opportunity to escape, and even if she didn't her sentence was restricted to the weekend—if she could survive that long in Simon Herries' company, she reflected grimly. Perhaps it would sweeten the pill a little if she kept telling herself that he was hating her presence every bit as much as she hated his. Arrogant bully! she thought resentfully, kidnapping her, dragging her down here, refusing to listen to her, or give her a chance to explain.

Still fuming, her tired body forced her mind to relinquish its hold on reality, and sleep stole over her.

CHAPTER FOUR

WHEN India opened her eyes she couldn't remember where she was. All she could see was the pattern cast by the sun shining through the barred window, and her heart started to thump in slow terror until she realised that she was not literally imprisoned in some cell but merely an unwilling occupant of Simon Herries' nursery.

Nursery! For the first time she was able to examine her surroundings in daylight, and what she saw made her wrinkle her nose in disgust.

The walls were painted a uniform beige which had turned to grubby grey in places. A thin thread-bare rug, as unlike her Persian rug as it was possible to be, was the sole floor covering, shabby, faded curtains hanging at the windows. To India the whole room was depressing. Pity the poor children who had had to endure it, she reflected, sliding out of the bed and padding across to the window, hitching up the over-long pyjamas as she did so.

In any other circumstances the view from the bedroom would have enchanted her. Born and bred in Cornwall, she missed the countryside and the sea. There was no churning, fascinating Atlantic here, but mile after mile of rolling fields, pale green with the tiny shoots of spring crops; the sky a pale duck egg blue. A primrose yellow sun shone down on the garden below; a tangle of honeysuckle and old-fashioned roses climbing upwards towards her dormer window and the ancient tiles above it.

If this house were hers she would tear down these bars, and make a feature out of the small bay window; a covered seat perhaps, with a hinged lid to accommodate children's toys; pretty Laura Ashley cottons, or her favourite Tissunique from Liberty's; polished floorboards; fresh cane furniture ... She was so absorbed in mentally refurbishing the room that she almost forgot what she was doing in it. Almost—but not quite.

A glance from the bedroom window had been enough to assure her that even if it had not been barred she couldn't possibly have climbed to freedom from it.

Securing her borrowed pyjamas with one hand, she headed for the door. Trust Simon Herries to point out that the pyjamas had never been worn. For one second she had a disturbing mental image of his body without the civilising influence of sophisticated clothes. Her heart seemed to stand still, the blood leaving her face, only to rush back in a wave of fierce colour, as logic fought against instinct. Why, when all the other men she had met in her twenty-five years had left her cool, if not cold, did she suddenly have to react like this to a man she actively despised?

It must be his sheer physical charisma, she decided weakly, refusing to acknowledge the power of her traitorous thoughts, and reaching for the door with her free hand.

To her amazement it opened. Without stopping to think she stepped forward, coming to an abrupt halt as she found her eyes on a level with the tanned column of Simon Herries' throat. Wildly she glanced downwards—a mistake; the terry robe which appeared to be his only covering was merely belted loosely around the waist, revealing several inches of tanned flesh against which a sprinkling of dark hairs curled and through which he was pushing his fingers idly, rubbing the taut flesh beneath.

Deep down inside her India felt something quiver into life; a heated melting sensation of which she had no prior experience. Dragging her eyes away from Simon Herries' body, she looked upwards, and saw to her consternation that he was regarding her with eyes whose expression told her that he was sardonically aware of her reaction.

Heat scorched through her, starting in the pit of her stomach and spreading outwards until there was not a part of her unaware of it. She started to tremble, reaching instinctively for the door, and instead found that her groping fingers were clutching the solid muscle of Simon Herries' arm.

'Thinking of going somewhere?'

'Dressed like this?'

If she had hoped to emulate his sardonically dry tones, she had failed, because instead of catching him off guard they merely drew wryly appraising eyes to the full roundedness of her breasts and the slender line of her thighs beneath the borrowed pyjamas.

'It might cause quite a stir,' he agreed mockingly, 'but I shouldn't have thought a little thing like that would deter you ... Not that you would have got very far. The garage is locked, as are the doors, and I have the keys. Unless of course you were planning to enter my room and make a search.'

Somehow the way he drawled the words imbued them with a sexuality that left India burning from head to toe with furious resentment, her fingers curling instinctively into the terry towelling.

All her good intentions of saying and doing nothing to further antagonise him but merely to endure the weekend as best she could, and once it was over put it safely behind her were forgotten. Her eyes kindling she took a deep breath.

'Why . . .'

'Simon? You up yet?'

Iron fingers clamped over her mouth, dark grey eyes warning her not to speak, and then to India's horror the pleasant feminine voice continued hesitantly, 'Mel's with me. He's just arrived home. Can we come up?'

The moment she heard Melford's name uttered India stiffened.

Without replying to the woman who India took to be Alison, Mel's wife, Simon Herries grasped India's wrist, pulling her quickly along the short distance between her room and his, and thrusting her inside, his hand still over her mouth.

He had moved so quickly that India hadn't had the opportunity to resist, but as he released her, quickly spinning her round, she made the most of her freedom, and darted towards the door, no firm purpose in mind save escape from the grimly determined look she saw in Simon's eyes.

She had barely taken two paces when her arm was seized with a grip that rocked her back on her heels, and taking momentary advantage of her unsteadiness, Simon used his superior weight to force her backwards on to the rumpled bed, pinning her there with the hardness of his body.

India could hear footsteps on the stairs, a puzzled

female voice saying uncertainly, 'I'm sure he said it was this weekend he was coming down. Mrs Barton told me yesterday she'd stocked up the fridge for him.'

'Perhaps he's gone out; visiting one of his lady-friends. You know Simon.'

India closed her eyes as she recognised Mel's familiar tones.

When she opened them again Simon Herries was watching her without compassion or any other emotion save for a cold, clinical detachment which sent danger signals flashing in her brain.

They both heard the hand on the door handle at the same time. India closed her eyes again, shivering and tense, gasping with shock as with one ruthless movement Simon ripped open her pyjama jacket, exposing the quivering swell of her breasts, her skin smooth and pale, and delicately rose-pink-tipped.

Her cry of protest was lost beneath hard male lips, that dominated and abused, bruising the soft inner flesh of her mouth, as lean, cruel fingers bruised her upper arms, the rough scrape of his body hair rasping against her breasts as he forced her down against the mattress.

Panic and hysteria fought equally for supremacy as India arched her back convulsively, trying to escape the suffocating intensely male presence; the alien intrusion of fingers which cupped her breast with shameless disregard for who might observe him, as the bedroom door was pushed open and a small, dark woman, followed by Melford Taylor, entered the room.

For a moment there was simply silence; and then both Alison and Melford spoke together, Alison apologising—not to India, but to Simon; who had made a brief parody of shielding India from their eyes by pulling a corner of a sheet over her exposed breasts— that neither Alison nor Mel were deceived by this gentlemanly gesture was patently obvious from the faint pink tinge to Alison's creamy skin, and the grey, haunted expression in Mel's eyes as he studiously avoided looking at India.

'You might have knocked,' Simon Herries said easily. 'What brings you here at this ungodly hour of the day anyway?' Without giving his cousin an opportunity to reply he added casually, 'Oh, by the way, meet India. India, my cousin Alison and her husband Mel. It's okay, Mel, no one expects you to shake hands in the circumstances,' he added sardonically, as Mel stepped forward and then back, his face haggard. 'After all, they hardly warrant any formality.'

'We came to see if you fancied lunch at the Plough and Flail,' Alison said quickly. 'But of course . . .'

'Sounds great,' Simon interrupted smoothly, his fingers lacing tightly with India's in a painful reminder of the fact that she was at his mercy.

'We'll enjoy it, won't we, darling? Besides, it will save you having to make lunch.'

'I don't mind,' India protested huskily, unable to bear the thought of Mel's reproachful eyes on her all through lunch. 'I'll enjoy cooking for you . . .'

God, how it hurt to force the lies from her aching throat, but there was no other alternative.

Simon's laugh scorched her skin, his lips nuzzling the side of her throat where a pulse throbbed betrayingly, his voice soft and falsely indulgent as he murmured,

'Don't waste your energy, I can think of far more entertaining ways of passing the time, can't you?'

'Can't you see you're embarrassing the poor girl?' Alison criticised him bracingly, smiling briefly at India.

'*I'm* embarrassing her?' The dark eyebrows shot upwards. 'My dear Alison, I wasn't the one who came bursting in here, interrupting us almost on the point of . . .'

'Yes, well, I'm sorry about that,' Alison interrupted hastily, tucking her arm through Mel's. 'It was just that I couldn't wait to tell you that Mel was back.'

'Well, now you've told me, okay?'

'See you at the Plough at one? Sorry about the intrusion. India—what an unusual name . . .' Alison added.

'My father chose it. He was an engineer and was working there when I was born,' India explained, hating herself for the way in which the guilty colour seeped up under her skin. What did it matter what this woman thought of her? She wasn't likely to see her ever again, and what if she did? These were the 1980s, no one thought twice about unmarried couples sleeping together. But she and Simon Herries weren't a 'couple' in the recognised sense of the word; and it cut her to the bone to be seen as the type of easy lay who repaid a pleasant evening out with a night in bed. And then there was Mel. Since he had entered the room he had been avoiding India's eyes; and she could hardly bring herself to look at him. What on earth must he be thinking? Although he had never pressed her sexually he had desired her, and she had pleaded an aversion to casual affairs; or indeed to any affairs, especially with married men. Simon Herries wasn't married, of course, but as far as Mel knew she didn't know Simon from Adam. Suddenly she remembered the last time they had dined together, and she had mentioned Simon to Mel. He had an opportunity then to tell her that he was Alison's cousin, but instead he had pretended only a casual acquaintance. She prided herself on not being the vain type of woman who delighted on keeping men on a string, always promising but never delivering, but it was unpalatable to think of Mel leaving this house in the belief that she had spent the night with Simon. At the first opportunity she would set the record straight, she promised herself. Mel had surely known her long enough to believe her above Simon Herries.

'Until lunchtime, then. Don't worry, we'll let ourselves out,' Alison assured them.

'Sorry to have interrupted your "fun",' Mel added in a voice that shook with fury and bitterness, his eyes dark with pain as he averted them from the sight of India's body more revealed than concealed by the thin cotton sheet.

When he reached the door, a wild impulse to call him back and explain overwhelmed India, but as though he had read her mind, Simon bent his head, his fingers grasping her wrists, his mouth against hers as he drawled huskily,

'Close the door behind you, will you, Mel, and tell Alison to lock up after her. I don't want any more interruptions!'

'Don't try anything,' he warned India as the door closed. 'It wouldn't do any good anyway. Not exactly what I'd planned, but effective nonetheless.

There's nothing quite so damning as the evidence one sees with one's own eyes—after all, we all know that seeing is believing, don't we?'

'How could you?' she protested in a thick, choked voice that shook with emotion. 'How could you do such a thing . . .?'

'Quite easily,' came the prompt rejoinder. 'Quite easily,' he reiterated in a different tone, and India froze as she realised that his eyes were resting on the slender shape of her body beneath the sheet. 'Oh, it's all right,' he assured her grimly. 'Physically you might be alluring, all creamy skin and enticing curves, but while my body might find momentary physical satisfaction in possessing yours, I'm no longer a teenager who finds physical relief sufficient in its own right—I look for something else in a woman—tenderness, the ability to give something of herself.'

'And you—what do you give in turn?' India demanded unwisely. 'Nothing worth treasuring, if the gossip columns are anything to go by—the average life of your relationships is something like a handful of months, isn't it; enough for *your* physical abilities to begin to pall.'

'What are you hoping for—a demonstration?' Simon Herries sneered. 'Oh, come on,' he added contemptuously. 'I saw how you were looking at me earlier on. What's the problem—can't Mel satisfy you?'

Words of hot denial trembled on India's lips, only to be swallowed as she realised the futility of protesting her innocence, or explaining that it was not him she had reacted to, merely the proximity of any male in such emotive circumstances. She might just as well try to convince him that Mel was not her lover, India acknowledged tiredly; that there had been no lovers; that he was the closest she had come to intimacy of the sort he obviously took for granted; that she had been so busy furthering her career that she was still a virgin.

'You can use the bathroom first,' Simon told her.

'What am I going to wear?' India murmured half to herself, suddenly remembering that the only clothes she had were her evening dress and these pyjamas.

In answer to her query, Simon swung himself up off the bed and pulled open one of the doors of a row of expensive fitted wardrobes which blended perfectly into the room.

'Try these,' he suggested, throwing a pair of faded denims on to the bed. 'And this . . .' A checked shirt followed the jeans. India hadn't realised how suspiciously she was staring at them until Simon said dryly. 'Forget it; they belong to Rick—Alison's brother.' He left them here one day when he was helping me work on the house. My daily must have found them and washed them out, since when they've been hanging in my wardrobe.'

India didn't linger in the bathroom. The jeans, although tight, fitted, as did the shirt, but she avoided looking at her shapely outline, still too disturbed by the events of the morning.

'How about some breakfast?' Simon suggested when she emerged from the bathroom. 'You'll find everything you need in the fridge. I take it you *can* cook?'

It was on the tip of her tongue to deny it, but

what was the point? Besides, she herself was hungry, much to her amazement.

'And don't try anything,' Simon warned her. 'All the doors are locked, and the keys are right here.' He patted the pocket of his robe. 'And you can forget about the telephone too. There's an extension in my bedroom, and I'll be able to hear if you lift the receiver. If you do, what happened this morning will be nothing compared to what I *can* do.'

With that threat ringing in her ears, India made her way downstairs. She had been considering ringing for a taxi while Simon was in the bathroom, but what was the point of risking a possible scene? He had achieved his purpose; he had nothing more to gain from keeping her here, and she intended to tell him so. As for Mel . . . A lump of misery lodged in India's throat as she remembered the look of utter disbelief on his face. Perhaps in the end it was better this way, she acknowledged; better for him to have a concrete reason for despising her; that way he would be able to put her behind him all the more easily, and if the papers were anything to go by her own reputation was hardly likely to suffer if her name was ever coupled with Simon Herries, she thought cynically as she busied herself removing eggs, bacon, sausages and tomatoes from the fridge. There was even a basket full of mushrooms, and soon the kitchen was full of the mouthwatering smell of frying bacon.

'Very domesticated!'

Engrossed in her task, she hadn't heard Simon enter the kitchen. His hair was still damp from the shower, the lean jaw which earlier had rasped against her own tender flesh was now freshly shaved; jeans and a checked shirt similar to her own did little to mask the powerful masculine structure of his body as he bent to open a cupboard and removed a loaf of bread, deftly cutting off several slices.

'Why the surprise? Every man ought at least to know the rudiments of cooking,' he told her, 'if only in the interests of self-preservation. I don't pretend to be a Cordon Bleu, but I can manage the basics.'

'I was thinking,' India began, bending over the bacon to conceal her expression from him, 'now that your plan has worked so well, and Mel has seen me with you, couldn't I just go back to London?'

'And have Alison and Mel wondering why? Oh no. I want it firmly fixed in Mel's mind that you've transferred your allegiance to me . . .'

'Don't you think you're taking a risk? I could tell him the truth.'

'You could try . . .' he drawled.

'What are you hoping to do? Appeal to the better side of my nature by forcing me to watch him with Alison?'

'What better side? I'm a realist, not a romantic. If I'd thought for a minute that I could have persuaded you to give up Mel simply by telling you about Alison, do you think for one moment that I wouldn't have done? Oh no, my dear, I want it firmly fixed in Mel's mind that you're a fickle, false character; a heartbreaker and home-wrecker whom he's better off without.'

'Well, we're here. Out you get!'

The Ferrari wasn't the only car parked on the forecourt of the low stone-built pub when they drew up outside it shortly after one o'clock.

Simon parked next to a Range Rover, which he

told India belonged to Alison and Mel. 'They find it useful during the schoolholidays. They used to go to France every year, to an old farmhouse in Provence.'

Another unsubtle reminder of Mel's family obligations? India refused to be drawn.

Several of the men standing at the bar glanced admiringly at her tall, slender figure in her borrowed jeans as they walked into the pub. A large pale cream labrador rose from the floor with obvious difficulty and waddled over to sniff India's outstretched fingers assessingly, and rub her head dotingly against Simon.

'Never trust a man who doesn't like animals,' her father had been fond of saying, but obviously even fathers could be wrong.

Alison and Mel were waiting for them at a table by one of the small leaded windows, and India's startled upward glance when Simon slipped his arm round her waist brought an extremely saturnine expression to his eyes, as he looked down at her in a parody of tenderness and murmured softly,

'We are supposed to be lovers, remember.'

The casual manner in which he referred to the incident earlier in the day, which still had the power to bring burning colour to India's cheeks, made her respond icily,

'Really? Do you always make a habit of molesting your women friends in public?'

'Oh, hardly that,' he drawled in response. 'But don't tempt me. Something tells me that you're the type of woman it would be fatally easy to respond to with physical anger.'

They had drawn level with Alison and Mel. India

felt as though her face were frozen in a mask of rage, her fingers curled tightly into her palms. *She* was the victim of this unnecessary charade; she was the one who had been insulted and reviled, almost to the point of physical abuse, and yet he talked of him being roused to physical anger!

'Tell me a little about yourself,' Alison invited ten minutes later when Simon and Mel had gone to make arrangements for their lunch. As Simon had been standing up at the time it would have been quite natural for him to go alone, but instead he had suggested that Mel accompany him. Making sure she wasn't given the opportunity to tell him the truth? India wondered.

Dragging her mind off Simon, she tried to concentrate on Alison. In other circumstances she could have liked the other woman, who was quite different from the wife she had envisaged from Mel's conversation.

'There's very little to tell . . .' she began.

Alison laughed goodnaturedly. 'I'm sorry. Mel's always telling me I'm too nosey. Well, tell me how you came to meet Simon, then . . .'

'We were introduced by an acquaintance,' India replied with perfect truth.

'And he fell madly in love with you and you with him! You're the first girl he's ever brought down here and actually introduced to the family, you know.'

It was on the tip of India's tongue to point out that 'introduce' was hardly the word she would have used to describe the morning's contretemps, but as though she sensed her embarrassment Alison said quite easily,

'I'm sorry about this morning. Simon's house-keeper didn't tell me he was bringing anyone down with him. I wanted to tell him that the boys are home for the weekend—they're both at boarding school—I wanted to invite him over for dinner tonight. He's James' godfather, and both of them dote on him. He's been so good to them.'

'He told me how fond he was of you,' India agreed noncommittally.

'Did he?' Alison smiled. 'Really we're more like brother and sister than cousins. He spent most of his holidays with my parents, you know. His own parents divorced when he was nine.' For a moment her face clouded over, and then she smiled again. 'A very bad age, I think; old enough to be aware of the undercurrents but too young to make allowances for adult emotions. For a while he was very bitter; he refused to have anything to do with his mother for several years. She's dead now and I believe he's grateful for the fact that he had the opportunity to make things up with her before she and her second husband were killed. She was the one to break up the marriage, you see. She was never really cut out to be the wife of a country farmer—which was really what Simon's father was—I suppose years ago they'd have been called "landed gentry"——' she pulled a slight face. 'He adored Louise. He died shortly after she left him—overwork, the doctor called it, but I can remember Simon saying that his mother had killed him. Poor little thing; he flatly refused to go to the funeral. In fact it was weeks before my parents could get him to accept that John had gone. The estate had to be sold, of course; there were heavy debts. Fortunately there was enough left to put

Simon through school and later university, but he'd changed; become not exactly bitter—wary, I think would be the best description, which is why we've all been holding our breath hoping that eventually he would find the right girl—the one who can break through that tough outer crust he assumes.'

What with? India found herself thinking. A pick-axe? Dynamite?

'I haven't known him very long,' she said cautiously, aware that Alison was expecting some response from her. In some ways she could appreciate Simon's desire to protect his cousin, in view of what she had told her, and her frank, confiding manner; unlike Simon, Alison was far from careful and cautious.

'No, but I can see that you're different from his other girl-friends,' Alison told her earnestly.

'What are you two discussing so seriously?'

India hadn't seen Simon and Mel approaching their table, and she stiffened instinctively.

'Nothing,' Alison replied airily. 'I was just telling her that she's different from your normal run of girls.'

'You're so right,' Simon agreed softly, his eyes on India's over-bright eyes and trembling mouth. 'You haven't been exchanging any more secrets, have you?'

His hand slid along her shoulder and up into her hair, forcing India's head back so that she had to look up at him.

India knew what he meant. He wanted to know if she had told Alison the truth. To punish him she said lightly, 'Alison came over this morning to ask if you wanted to have dinner with them tonight.'

'Yes, why don't you?' Alison interrupted eagerly. 'The boys are both home, and they're longing to see you . . . both of you must come.'

'I'm afraid I can't,' India apologised, smiling with false sweetness at Simon and pulling a wry face. 'Honestly, darling, I know every girl admires impetuosity in a lover, but sweeping me off here with nothing to wear apart from the clothes I stood up in!—a very inappropriate evening dress and cloak,' she told Alison.

'Simon did that?' Alison enquired with delight. 'Never!'

'Indeed he did. Positively kidnapped me,' India told her with another saccharine smile in Simon's direction. While her pride exulted fiercely in the murderous look she saw in his eyes, part of her noted with dismay the clenching of his jaw, and the hard tightening of his mouth as his eyes held hers.

'You gave me no option,' he answered truthfully, the hand he had wound into her hair sliding down to the base of her neck where the lean fingers exerted a pressure which made her want to cry out aloud with pain.

'Besides, I'm tired of sharing you with other people. I wanted you all to myself.'

Mel had remained silent throughout this exchange, but suddenly he said abruptly,

'They're signalling that our table's ready.'

'I don't think Simon and India are particularly hungry,' Alison giggled, 'at least not for food. Looking at you two makes me feel quite envious,' she told India with a sigh, before turning to Mel to say softly, 'Do you remember when you couldn't bear to let me out of your sight; when you had to take that trip to Paris on business and you refused because it was our first wedding anniversary?'

Embarrassed at being forced to witness this small exchange, India glanced away, and immediately wished she hadn't as she encountered the grimly aware look in Simon Herries' eyes.

Lunch was a mainly silent affair, after which Simon announced abruptly that he had changed his mind about the weekend and had decided that they ought to return to London almost straight away.

'Oh, but . . .' Alison protested, falling silent, as she realised that no one else was supporting her protest. 'Well, if you must,' she said lamely. 'But next time you come down give us some warning—and bring India with you. I definitely approve,' she added irrepressibly.

After that the remainder of the afternoon passed in a haze, India was aware of them taking their leave of Alison and Mel; Mel's fingers trembling against hers as they shook hands, his face unnaturally pale; she was also aware of Alison's bright chatter, filling an aching silence when she suggested that the four of them go out for a meal together some time, but the return journey to the house to pick up her clothes seemed to be part of a dream world she had suddenly started inhabiting.

Simon drove back to London in almost complete silence, broken only when he said curtly at one point,

'Women like you amaze me. On the face of it you and Alison were getting on like a house on fire, and yet underneath you've been planning to steal her husband; I wonder how she would have treated you if she'd known that!'

'It's not true!' India protested. 'I'm not . . .'

'No? Oh, of course,' Simon agreed sarcastically, 'you haven't done anything to influence Mel; you haven't made him aware of you; of your youth and vitality, or your body . . .' His eyes slid down the slender length of her legs in the tight jeans. 'What did you tell her when the two of you were alone?' he asked abruptly.

'Not that I was having an affair with her husband,' India replied just as acidly. 'As a matter of fact we talked most about you. She was telling me how close you were as children.'

After that no conversation passed between them until Simon stopped the car outside India's flat, by which time dusk was falling over the city.

'Why did you decide to bring me back?' India queried as she opened the door.

'Not because I couldn't trust myself to spend a night alone with you without wanting to possess you,' she was told brutally. 'What was the point in staying? The purpose of our visit had been accomplished. It was a stroke of luck that Mel should be home for the weekend, or don't you agree?' he asked sardonically.

'As a matter of fact, I do,' India agreed, exulting in the pleasure of having surprised him for once. 'It means that I have to spend less time as your prisoner. Goodbye,' she added formally. 'I wish I could say that it's been a pleasure knowing you, but we both know that I'd be lying.'

CHAPTER FIVE

'How was the party?' Jenny asked her on Monday morning, while she examined the mail. 'Umm, there's a note here from Ursula Blanchard . . .' she pulled a face. 'I don't know what it is about that woman, but she really gets my back up. She's so unbelievably snooty!'

'That's what comes of being a top model who married money,' India supplied dryly, glad of the opportunity to avoid discussing the events of the weekend.

'Umm, she's divorced, isn't she?' Jenny added, frowning suddenly. 'Wasn't she Simon Herries' girl-friend before he took up with Melisande? I'm sure I remember reading an article in one of the glossies about her; in the days when she was pretty sure that she was going to be Mrs Simon Herries.'

India, who had stiffened instinctively at the mention of Simon Herries' name, relaxed, and forced a careless smile.

'I honestly don't know. What does she say?'

In response Jenny passed the letter over. It stated quite simply that the ex-model intended to call on them to discuss the possibility of them designing a gown for her to wear to a charity gala to which she had been invited.

'We're honoured,' Jenny commented to India. 'All we've done for her before is the odd skirt, isn't it?'

'Umm, she normally goes for the big name labels.'

'She would,' Jenny opined nastily. 'Shall I give her a ring and fix an appointment?'

Agreeing, India made her escape before her secretary could question her further on the 'party' she was supposed to have attended. Now that she was back at work, enveloped in the relative security of routine, the weekend had taken on a hazy, almost unreal aspect, rather like a bad dream fuzzily remembered, with just the odd isolated incident remaining crystal sharp; like those moments in Simon Herries' bedroom, before Alison had thrust open the door, when for the briefest measure of time India had actually felt her flesh react in instinctive female response to the masculinity of her captor.

Dragging her thoughts away from Simon Herries, she tried to concentrate on her work, but this proved easier said than done. Against her will she found herself remembering what Alison had told her about his childhood. He didn't deserve her pity, she chided herself, not after what he had done to her. He was not the only child to suffer from the effects of a broken marriage . . . and yet something in Alison's telling of the plaintive story had touched an answering chord within her; a memory of how it had felt to realise that one's parents were not the happy, united unit one had so carefully believed.

Just before lunch the telephone rang. Jenny answered it, covering the receiver to whisper, 'It's Mel.'

'I'll take it in my own office,' India told her. 'Put him through, will you.'

She had been dreading this ever since her return, knowing that Mel would never simply leave matters as they stood.

'India?' His voice, sharp with anxiety and shock, made her instantly aware of how he had looked at her on Saturday morning. 'Are you all right?'

The weakness which had filled her at the initial sound of his voice faded, a new strength of purpose taking its place as she grasped the phone so tightly that her knuckles showed white through her pale skin.

'Of course I am,' she replied lightly. 'Why on earth shouldn't I be?'

There was silence, as though her reply had somehow thrown him, and then he said hoarsely,

'For God's sake, India, what the hell's going on? One minute you're telling me that there's just no way that you would get involved with me, whatever your feelings, and the next I discover that you're my brother-in-law's latest conquest.'

'But that's quite different,' India protested, purposely misunderstanding his question. 'Simon isn't married, and doesn't have commitments elsewhere.'

For a few seconds India thought she had got away with it, and then Mel said softly,

'Come on, India, I'm not that much of a bad judge of character. I know you, and telling me that just won't wash. You yourself told me your views on bed-hopping, and I know you well enough to bet all I own on the fact that you aren't the kind of girl to change overnight.'

Her palm was sticky, the receiver damp where she had been clinging to the phone. Here it was, her chance to tell Mel the truth and completely expose Simon. But if she did that mightn't some of the blame—completely unjustifiably—rebound on to

Alison, who India was quite positive had known nothing of her cousin's machinations?

'India, are you still there?'

She thought quickly, and made up her mind.

'Yes, I'm still here, but there's something you don't understand. I wouldn't have an affair with you partially because you were married, and partially because I didn't love you—not the way I love Simon.'

There, it was out; done for better or for worse. She started to tremble with reaction, sensing Mel's bitter frustration reaching out across the telephone wires to reach her.

'You love him? I didn't even know you knew him apart from meeting at the restaurant.'

'It's true,' India said quietly. 'Melisande introduced us. I suppose you could just say it was one of those things.'

'It must have been, to have got you into bed with him so quickly,' Mel said brutally. 'Perhaps I ought to ask him what aftershave he uses. God, and to think I thought you were different!'

India's fingernails were digging into her palms, with the effort of forcing herself not to admit to the truth, the sarcasm in Mel's voice lacerating her pride like a lash.

'I'm sorry, Mel,' she said quietly, adding mentally, *more sorry than you realise, and I only hope to God I'm doing the right thing.*

'Not half as much as I am. No wonder you told me to stay with Alison!'

'She's a charming person.'

'Yes,' he agreed heavily, 'and I'm just beginning to realise what I might have thrown away, and all

for the sake of something my dear brother-in-law
has had simply for the asking. India!' he demanded
sharply. 'Are you still there?'

'Yes,' she answered bleakly, 'but I don't think
we've got anything more to say to one another, do
you, Mel?'

'No. Just tell me one thing,' he demanded harshly.
'Does Simon know about us?'

India thought hurriedly, wondering what to say
for the best.

'He knows we know one another,' she hedged at
last. 'He saw us at the restaurant.'

'And it never occurred to you how he might react
if he discovered how I felt about you?'

'I don't believe it would make the slightest difference,' she responded truthfully.

There was a pause and then Mel said heavily, 'I
guess you're right. Goodbye then, India. I can't
honestly say I'm happy for you, or that I believe
that Simon is the right man for you. His affairs aren't
renowned for their longevity, you know,' he told her
curtly. 'What will you do when it's over?'

'Worry about it when it happens,' India said
lightly.

She was still sitting staring into space ten minutes
later when Jenny knocked on the door and said
urgently,

'Her Highness is here—Ursula Blanchard—and
she wants to see you—now.'

Lifting her eyebrows, India followed her secretary
into the salon where a tall, elegant blonde was
pacing the floor, her eyes hard as she swung round
and stared at India.

'I want to speak to you,' she began without preamble. 'Alone.'

When Jenny had whisked herself out of the salon, India invited Ursula to sit down, but the blonde ignored the invitation, turning on India instead, her eyes blazing with rage, as she glanced disdainfully over India's face.

'My God!' she exclaimed theatrically, giving another disbelieving look at India. 'Even now I can't believe it. It can't be for real!'

'Perhaps if you told me what you're talking about,' India suggested, hurriedly casting her mind back to the last outfit they had made for the ex-model. It was all of six months ago now, a very simple skirt, hardly the cause of all this emotion.

'I'm talking about Simon!' Ursula hissed at her. 'As if you didn't know. He must have lost his wits . . . He's always been renowned for the beauty of his girl-friends.'

'Thanks,' India replied dryly, 'but I'm not . . .'

'Don't lie to me!' Ursula demanded furiously. 'I bumped into Alison on Saturday and she told me all about it. How pleased she was that Simon had found a nice girl at last.' Her lip curled. 'A nice girl and Simon! You won't be able to keep him,' she told India. 'You'll see . . .'

'Who says I want to?' India interrupted mildly.

Ursula's eyebrows rose contemptuously. 'Of course you do, all girls like you always play for keeps, but this time you're playing in the wrong league, my dear. Simon wants a wife who can match him for sophistication; who moves in the same circles, not a little dressmaker, who knows no one.'

India swallowed hard on her growing anger.

'Don't you think Simon himself is the best judge of what he wants?' she asked in a deceptively soft voice.

'I know what he wants,' Ursula replied arrogantly. 'He wants me. He always has done. Why else do you think Lee divorced me?'

'What are you trying to tell me?' India asked evenly. 'That you and Simon were lovers?' She shrugged coolly, marvelling at her own ability to play-act. 'Simon's a sophisticated man in his mid-thirties—I'd hardly expect to be the only woman in his life. But what is past is past . . .' She was beginning to enjoy herself as she saw the ex-model's face drop and then harden with determination. 'And aren't you forgetting about Melisande?' she added lightly. 'If I'm going to be visited by every single one of Simon's ex's, I can see that I'm going to have a very busy time indeed!'

'You'll be sorry for this!' Ursula hissed as she flounced out. 'Simon took up with Melisande to punish me, that's all . . . You might have the approval of that idiot cousin of his, but Simon goes his own way—no one dictates to him.'

'I know.'

India said it with such quiet emphasis that the older woman went white with anger, her eyes as hard as pebbles as she directed a final bitter look at India before leaving the salon.

'What was all that about?' Jenny asked curiously later on. 'I could hear Her Highness raising her voice . . .'

'She wanted to warn me off Simon Herries,' India said dryly. 'She brings a whole new meaning to the words "predatory female".'

'Simon Herries is better off without her,' Jenny opined. 'Honestly, I can't imagine what he ever saw in her.' She did a double take. 'What did you say? She wanted to warn *you* off? But . . .'

'Don't ask,' India implored. 'It's a long and extremely complicated story, and suffice it to say that she was barking up the wrong tree; in fact there were moments when the sheer ludicrousness of the situation almost had me completely ruining Ursula's big scene by bursting out laughing!'

The next morning, however, when Jenny silently pointed out to her an article in one of the gossip columns, laughing was the last thing India felt like.

There in bold type was her name, and Simon Herries'. Simon Herries had found himself a new lady-love, the story read; and moreover one who was hotly tipped to become the first Mrs Herries. Family approval of the candidate had been sought, and all that was now awaited was a formal announcement.

'Ursula!' India groaned.

'She didn't?' Jenny protested in awed accents. 'My God, she must have been furious! Well, she's well and truly burned her boats now.' The phone rang and she reached for the receiver. 'This will be your intended,' she whispered mischievously to India. 'He's been on twice already, while you were on your way. Perhaps he wants to whisper sweet nothings!'

'Whisper' was hardly the operative word, India reflected as the ice-cold tones of Simon's voice washed over her like water straight off a glacier.

'Is this your idea of a joke?' he demanded without preamble, 'giving the gossip columns that choice item about our "relationship"?'

'What makes you so sure it was me?' India enquired, keeping a tight rein on her own anger, holding the receiver away from her ear as there was a sound like a combination of a snort and a curse.

'Who else would have the motive?'

'And if I were to tell you that it wasn't me?'

'Don't waste your breath,' came the hard reply. 'I suppose this is your way of getting even with me, is it?'

India was beginning to lose her temper—fast. 'Look,' she told him curtly, 'if you don't like it you can always print a disclaimer.'

'Don't think I wouldn't—if it weren't for one thing. By some misfortune my grandmother happens to have read the article. She was on the phone to me this morning demanding to know when she was going to get to meet the girl I'm thinking of marrying. It seems that Alison has already told her about you.'

'Tough luck,' India said coolly, without bothering to cloak her lack of sympathy. 'What am I supposed to do? Burst into tears?'

'What you're going to do is to visit my grandmother with me,' she was told tersely. 'It's all arranged. We're to dine with her tomorrow night.'

India had time to feel surprised that Simon Herries who had stamped roughshod over her feelings should have it in him to be so careful of his grandmother's before everything else was obliterated in a rush of rage as he added contemptuously, 'I'm quite positive that once she has met you, far from urging me to marriage as she has done these last five years, she'll be giving me the money to flee the country.'

In that moment India made up her mind. So Simon Herries wanted her to visit his grandmother, did he, and play the part of his supposed 'girl-friend', at the same time making quite clear his contempt and dislike of her personally. Very well then, she would play along with him, but if he thought she was going to allow him to get away with insulting her a second time, he had a shock in store! However, not wanting to make him suspicious, she forced doubt into her voice as she said slowly, 'But I don't understand. Why not simply tell your grandmother that it was all a mistake? After all, I'm not the first female to have her name linked publicly with yours.'

'True, but it just so happens that my grandmother has been trying to marry me off for years, plus the fact that she has a weak heart, and plus again that Alison has been singing your praises to her. So much so that I prefer her to see for herself exactly what you are.'

'And if I refuse to play along?'

She knew that he must have already anticipated her refusal and have come up with something to counteract it—a plea on behalf of his grandmother's ill-health perhaps, but when he did speak, what he had to say shocked India into disbelieving silence, her earlier anger a pale shadow of the rage she felt now as she digested his threat. If she refused he would personally ensure that her business reputation was so smeared that within six months she would find herself bankrupt. He could do it, he assured her, and she knew he was right. Her fingers clenched round the telephone, she said icily, taking a very deep breath, 'Very well, I agree.'

'Wise of you,' came the sardonic response. 'I've

already told Grandmother we'll dine with her to-morrow night at seven-thirty, I'll pick you up—be ready.'

There was a distinct click as he hung up, leaving India staring at the now silent receiver, her face pale, and her eyes half glazed with rage.

'You're the one who'll need to be ready, Simon Herries!' she promised grittily under her breath, as she slowly replaced the receiver.

India dressed for her meeting with Simon's grand-mother with great care.

Since making her decision a strange calm seemed to have come over her, but India herself was not deceived, and she knew quite well that beneath her calm, the temper that few people realised she posses-sed was simmering and bubbling, just waiting for the opportunity to erupt into lava-like rage.

She decided to wear one of her favourite black velvet dresses with a demure lace collar in soft cream. When she was ready she studied her reflection care-fully. The subdued make-up she was wearing em-phasised the green sparkle of her eyes, her hair brushing her shoulders in burnished curls, her mouth outlined in a warm burgundy coating of lip-gloss.

Simon arrived sharp on the dot of seven. India opened the door in silence, her coat already on. He glanced at her briefly, eyes resting inscrutably on her legs in their sheer black stockings for a brief span of time before moving upwards to study her face.

'Ready?' he asked at length.

India made no reply, simply preceding him through the door.

The Ferrari was parked outside. As before Simon

opened her door for her, making sure she was quite comfortable before walking round to the driver's side.

He had impeccable manners, India thought, she had to give him that. No doubt normally his dates enjoyed the sensation of being wrapped in masculine attention—in other circumstances she might have done so herself, because she had discovered that it was quite rare for girls as tall as herself to be treated with such courtesy.

It wasn't far to their destination. His grandmother had moved to London several years ago, Simon told her abruptly as he parked the car beneath an elegant block of flats.

India had not had much time to speculate too much on the woman she was going to meet—her mind had been too full of her plans for jolting Simon out of his arrogant complacency, and teaching him a lesson she sincerely hoped he would never forget, for that, but still it came as quite a shock to be greeted by a tiny, patently frail lady, who barely reached up to her shoulder, whose soft white hair was carefully arranged around a face which still bore traces of great beauty and whose eyes were still as darkly grey as her grandson's.

'Come on in, both of you,' she invited. 'Ellie is just putting the finishing touches to dinner. Give me your coats . . . Ellie has been with me since I was widowed twelve years ago,' she explained to India as they followed her through a small square hallway into a comfortable and attractively furnished lounge. 'Simon found her for me, and she's a real treasure, although she can be a bit of a martinet at times.'

'Because she needs to be,' a humorous voice

chimed in as a middle-aged woman walked into the room. 'Otherwise there'd be no stopping you, would there?'

India liked Ellie Roberts on sight. She reminded her very much of one of her favourite schoolmistresses.

'Dinner won't be long,' she told them. 'I'll serve it and then I'll leave you to it. I'm going to spend the evening with my sister.'

'Ellie doesn't get out enough,' Virginia Herries told India as Simon walked across the room and started to pour drinks. 'I tease her dreadfully at times, but I honestly don't know what I'd do without her. I can't believe sometimes that it's only twelve years since she first came to me—I feel as though we've known one another all our lives. Oh, Simon!' she exclaimed as he returned with a single glass of sherry which he gave to India. 'Don't I get one?'

'You know what Dr Mackay says Grandmother,' he said.

She pulled a face. 'David Mackay! He's an old woman!'

'Nevertheless, he is your doctor. Perhaps if you're very good we'll let you have half a glass of wine with dinner,' he added, relenting slightly, a smile of such tenderness crossing his face that India found herself holding her breath in awe. Never once in their brief acquaintance has she seen him smile quite like that, and the sight of that tender smile for some reason brought an unexpected lump to her throat an a vague ache to her heart for which she could find no rational explanation.

True to her word, once they had finished the delicious pâté she had prepared and had been served with steak stuffed with oysters and marinated in wine, Ellie took her leave of them.

'Dessert is in the kitchen,' she told Simon. 'No, don't get up, perhaps your young lady will see to the coffee?'

When India agreed, she smiled gratefully at her.

'Now, my dear,' Virginia Herries invited when they had finished the unbelievably light raspberry soufflé and were sitting drinking coffee while Simon helped himself to some Brie, 'tell me all about yourself.'

'There's nothing really to tell,' India protested, conscious of Simon's eyes hard on her face.

Virginia Herries laughed. 'Now that's patently a mistruth! For one thing, Alison tells me that you design the most enchanting clothes. Tell me about that.'

Briefly India outlined her career.

'You've done exceptionally well,' Virginia Herries told her. 'I like girls to have ambition, it proves that they are people in their own right. And the fact that you've been so successful proves that you have the talent to match.'

'Either that or the right kind of financial support,' Simon put in dryly, drawing a frown from his grandmother's face.

'Darling, you'll make your grandmother believe you don't have any faith in me,' India pouted, unable to believe until the words were out that she had actually had the audacity to put her plan into action. But it was too late to retract now. While his grandmother looked on indulgently, Simon was staring at her, with eyes suddenly sharpening with suspicion.

Let him think what he liked, India thought rebelliously; after all, he was the one who had accused her, condemned her—and quite wrongly. Her anger smouldered as she remembered his accusation that she had deliberately given the item to the gossip columnist out of spite. If she wanted revenge there were far subtler ways of achieving it, as she was now about to prove to him. Give a dog a bad name . . . she told herself as she tried to quell the small voice of sanity pleading with her to recant, cautioning that there were cases when prudence was more important than pride.

'Quite right,' Virginia Herries approved. 'Alison tells me that you took India down to the house, Simon . . .' She deliberately left the sentence unembroidered, but India's face flushed as she realised that the older woman might have been told about the unedifying scene Alison and Mel had interrupted. 'Of course,' she added hurriedly as her grandson's eyebrows rose mockingly, 'nowadays things are quite different, but in my day a young man didn't take a girl away unchaperoned unless they were engaged at the very least.'

'Things are different these days, Grandmother,' Simon said casually. 'And India is far from being the first girl I've taken down to Meadow's End.'

'I know, but India is different,' his grandmother argued, favouring India with a charming smile. 'And you obviously think so too!'

'I do?'

'Well, of course, otherwise you would never have allowed that item to appear in the papers.'

'Even I can't stop Fleet Street hacks from muckraking, Grandmother,' he told the older woman extremely dryly.

India took a deep breath. Here it was; her chance to show Simon Herries just what she could do when she tried!

'Oh, come along, darling,' she coaxed, leaning across to place her hand on his arm, her eyes wide and guileless as she stared up at him. 'Surely we don't need to keep our secret from your grandmother?'

There was no need for her to say any more. Simon's loaded. 'What?' was obliterated by Virginia Herries' excited, 'Darlings! I knew it! Simon, Ellie put some champagne in the fridge on my instructions—go and get it. We must drink to your future. Oh, I'm so excited!'

There was a pink tinge to her cheeks, a sparkle to her eyes that smote India to the heart, but this was no time to allow sentiment to outweigh logic. Simon had falsely branded her as the very worst type of female and he was getting no more than his just deserts, but when she had originally decided to play this trick on him, she had not allowed for the fact that she would be so drawn to his grandmother. How would she take it when she discovered that there was no 'engagement'? Telling herself firmly that that was Simon's problem, India sat back in her chair, veiling her eyes as he returned with the champagne, although she very nearly lost her resolve when, having poured three glasses, he brought his hand to rest on the back of her neck, the pressure of his fingers exerting a force which compelled her to look up at him. Standing beside her chair he seemed unpleasantly tall and overpowering. She had to swallow hard to dispel the thought that she would have been much, much wiser simply to accept things as they stood.

'Well, darling,'—was only she aware of the hard metallic inflection in the last word?—'it seems we're going to have to celebrate ahead of schedule after all.'

'Well, aren't you going to kiss her?'

India couldn't stop her eyes from widening fractionally, reflecting her dismay. This was something she hadn't bargained for.

As he bent towards her, strategically placing himself between her and his grandmother, so that the latter could only see his back view, he mouthed silently to India, 'I don't know what the hell you think you're playing at, but there's no way I'm going to let you get away with this!'

India's retort was stifled beneath a mouth which seemed to burn her own with the harshness of extreme cold, making her shudder violently as she tried to wrench her mouth away, her breathing stifled as the kiss was prolonged.

'Happy now?' he enquired of his grandmother, when India had at last been released. She longed to touch her mouth, to rub away the memory of that bitter contact, but dared not do so in front of the older woman.

'More than I can say,' the old lady replied tremulously, tears blurring her eyes. 'You can't know how I've longed and prayed for this, Simon. Now at last I know that you've put the past behind you, forgiven your mother.'

There was a small significant pause, while India remembered what Alison had told her about Simon's mother, and then he was saying calmly,

'Well, I have to think of Meadow's End, you know. Having re-purchased the estate, I'm going to need a son to inherit it from me, aren't I?'

'What will you do? Live in the present house for the time being? Alison told me that Meadow's End itself is coming along quite well. Has Simon shown you Meadow's End yet?' she asked India. 'The estate was sold after my son's death—something Simon has always regretted, I know, but of course the fire which prompted the previous owners to sell to Simon practically gutted the main house, which is why he's been living in what was once the farm manager's house.'

'She hasn't seen it yet,' Simon supplied, coming to stand behind India, his hands resting lightly on her shoulders. 'I didn't want to frighten her off before I proposed. Few girls would relish the prospect of taking on a husband who can only provide the burned out shell of a house as a home,' he joked.

'What about an engagement ring?' Virginia Herries demanded. 'And the wedding, when's that to be?'

'Give us time! We're barely engaged yet.'

'But there's no reason for you to wait.'

It was eleven o'clock before they finally left. Ellie, on her return, had to be appraised of the news, and more champagne drunk. India, who had a very low tolerance of alcohol, could feel her head beginning to swim as they emerged into the cold, frosty air, which was probably just as well, she reflected hazily, because the alcohol acted as an insulating blanket between her and the razor-sharp condemnation in Simon's eyes as he meticulously unlocked the car door for her, his eyes the colour of granite and just as hard, as he slid in beside her, closing the door with a cold precision which more than any number of words brought home to India the full enormity of what she had done.

'I suppose it's quite useless asking for an explanation,' he said at last. 'Or perhaps I can supply the answer for myself. You've lost Mel, your lover and financier, who better to take his place than the man who robbed you of him? And not just take his place, but provide the security of a rich husband. Is that what you were hoping for? That for my grandmother's sake I'd be forced to go through with this farce and then you could divorce me, claiming a large slice of my income? You don't know me,' he said hardily. 'As you're very soon going to find out. If you honestly thought I would fall for that ploy, my dear, you're either very naïve or an addict of romantic novelettes.'

India stared through her window, gritting her teeth. Was everything she did in connection with this man destined to be misinterpreted? How dared he think that she wanted him to marry her?

'For your information,' she told him angrily, 'marriage to you is the last thing I want.' Her lip curled scornfully. 'You've got far too big an idea of your own worth, Simon Herries; you're the last man I'd want as a husband! If you must know, the reason I allowed your grandmother to think we were engaged was simply to show you how it felt to be at the mercy of someone else's misinterpretation of circumstances. Furthermore, I did not tell the newspapers about us. The blame for that I suspect lies with one of your ex-girl-friends—Ursula Blanchard— who apparently learned from Alison that we spent the weekend together, and drew completely the wrong conclusions. I had to endure an hour of being called every unpleasant name under the sun before I could finally get rid of her. Neither have I ever been romantically involved with Mel. I like him, and I don't deny that he believes he is, or was, attracted to me, but I've never given him the slightest encouragement. Now, whether you believe me or not doesn't matter a damn to me, but I hope that tonight has shown you just how circumstances can be twisted to fit whatever explanation a person wants to give them. Your grandmother was already determined to believe that we were on the brink of an engagement . . .'

'And now she's convinced of it—thanks to you. Didn't it ever occur to you to think of the effect the truth is going to have on her when it comes out?' he demanded, completely ignoring her earlier comments. 'Or is it that you simply don't care?'

'Ought I to?' India asked hardily, preparing to escape from the car as they drew up outside her flat. 'Do you care about what you've done to me?'

'Oh no, not so fast . . .' he told her, reaching out and across her, her hair brushing his dark-suited shoulder as he locked the door. 'We have things to talk about, you and I.'

'Such as?'

'Such as our engagement. Oh, come on, surely you don't suppose for one minute that my grandmother will keep it to herself?' he demanded sarcastically. 'To save her face, if not my own, I'm going to have to play along—but only until I tell her the truth, so don't run away with the idea that you've won.'

'Won what?' India demanded furiously. 'You? My God!' she laughed bitterly. 'Some prize that would be! Hasn't it occurred to you that I just might be choosy about who I decide to spend the rest of my life with? That I might not want a man whose name has been linked with practically every little starlet and model in London?'

'You're exaggerating,' Simon said in bored accents. 'No woman really wants a man who's completely without experience.'

'Meaning you think I would find yours irresistible?' India shot back defiantly.

She knew she had gone too far when she saw the gleam in the dark grey eyes, and shrank back in her seat instinctively.

'Want me to prove it to you?' There was seduction and something else in the soft words; a kind of sure knowledge that aroused even while it repelled, filling her with an insane desire to possess the same knowledge and experience as the man next to her.

She made no demur as his arms came round her, her eyes wide open and her body quivering tensely as she waited for his kiss, but instead of possessing her mouth his lips were exploring the contours of her face, his thumbs slowly stroking the soft flesh of her throat until she ached with the tension of denying her body's response. It took all the willpower she possessed to prevent herself from turning her head until her lips met the hard male ones tracing a delicate line from her jaw to her eyelids. Her mouth felt dry, her heart thudding heavily against her ribs, emotions she had never experienced before making her aware of her own body in a manner she had previously thought only existed in the pages of a novel.

Then, when she had ceased to expect it, his mouth closed over hers, the fingers he had wound in her hair pulling her head back against his shoulder, exposing her lips to the experienced assault of his. A strange feeling began somewhere deep in the pit of her stomach and spread slowly throughout her body; a weak melting sensation that panicked her into stiffening instinctively against it, her eyes dilating in mingled shock and distress, her fingers clutching at the dark fabric of Simon's suit.

'Very good,' he drawled sardonically, releasing her. 'Only it just so happens that I'm not impressed by impressions of feigned virginity—no matter how excellent or artistic!'

CHAPTER SIX

THE phone rang and India reached for it.

'India! It's Alison. I had to ring you to tell you how thrilled Mel and I are by your news. Look, I have to come up to London this week. Why don't we all have dinner together? I'm dying to know your plans. I knew you were right for Simon the moment I saw you—well, the moment I saw you properly,' she amended with a chuckle. 'I hope you're going to make the wedding soon,' she added. 'In another three months I'm going to be huge, and both Mel and the doctor keep fussing dreadfully. Anyone would never think I'd had one baby before, never mind two! By the way, I've already spoken to Simon to tell him how pleased I am. In fact I think I'll give him another ring now and fix up this dinner date . . .'

She had rung off before India could protest, leaving her to reflect on the old saw that one lie leads to another. Oh well, she decided, Alison was Simon's cousin, it was up to him to deal with the problem. She refused to allow herself to remember how she had felt before staggering out of his car the night he had brought her home from his grandmother's. Purely physical reaction, she told herself, when the subject could no longer be ignored. Good heavens, she didn't even like the man! And yet he had definitely aroused her; touched something deep inside her that no other man had even approached doing.

Experience, India scoffed mentally, that was all it was. But the tiny knot of fear deep down inside her seemed to grow larger every day. And even though it was less than a week since that fateful dinner, she could still remember vividly everything about it, and what had followed.

Her phone rang again, she sighed and picked it up. As she had anticipated, it was Simon.

'Are you free on Saturday evening?' he asked her, much to her surprise. 'Alison is coming up to town and wants to dine with us.'

'Yes, she told me,' India agreed, feeling a little surprised that Simon had not found some way of discouraging Alison from making the journey. 'I don't think I am free,' she lied, glad that Simon couldn't see the tell-tale colour running up under her skin.

'Then cancel whatever you had on,' came the sharp retort. 'This whole mess was your doing, and you'll damn well play along with it now until I'm good and ready to finish it.'

'And if I don't?' India asked, amazed by her own apparent calm.

'My previous warning still stands. If you value your business, you'll do exactly what I say.'

'There's a word for men like you,' India said forcefully.

'And for women like you,' came the urbane reply. 'Don't forget—Saturday night. And for God's sake don't wear that velvet thing. It makes you look about sixteen.'

'What would you prefer me to wear?' India asked sarcastically, 'Something scarlet and skin-tight? You're out of touch, Simon Herries!'

Nevertheless when Saturday evening came, India deliberately chose to wear the cloth of gold dress again. It clung seductively to her body, making her aware of it in a way she had not known before.

Simon as always was prompt. He had booked a table at a restaurant India knew by reputation alone; she also knew, because Mel had once told her, that it was extremely difficult to get a table at anything less than a month's notice, unless one was a particular friend of the owner's.

Alison was already in the Ferrari when Simon escorted India out to it.

'Simon's spoiling me,' she said gaily to India. 'Honestly, anyone would think no one had ever had a baby before! Wait until you start,' she added, causing India to glance instinctively towards Simon. He was fastening his seat-belt, but he caught her look, his eyes grim as he drawled lightly,

'Give us time, Alison . . . I want India to myself for a little while first.'

It wasn't very far to the restaurant. They were ushered inside with flattering deference and shown to a table by the owner himself, whose name India was familiar with from the gossip columns.

'No need to ask what you want,' Simon said to Alison when they had all been handed menus.

She laughed and explained to India, 'Whenever I'm pregnant I always crave seafood. Quite right,' she told Simon. 'Seafood platter to start with.'

Simon ordered the pâté, and India, who was not feeling particularly hungry, due mainly to the tense state of her stomach nerves, settled for Florida cocktail. They were all having the speciality of the house for their main course, a Russian chicken dish, which when it came smelled mouthwateringly delicious.

To settle her nerves India drank her wine faster than she would normally have done, and didn't realise that the waiter had stepped forward to refill her glass until she raised it to her lips a second time.

The alcohol seemed to help, so she emptied the glass, a little startled to find the waiter at her elbow yet again.

From the very start of the evening she had been conscious of a certain brooding quality about Simon; a certain bitter expectancy that sawed on her own taut nerves. What did he expect? she asked herself angrily as Alison chattered brightly about her children and Mel. Had he honestly expected to get away with treating her as he had absolutely scot-free?

'You look absolutely gorgeous,' Alison confided to India over their sweet. 'That's a beautiful dress. One of your own?'

'Yes,' India admitted, 'but not designed for me. It was intended for a client who changed her mind, and rather than waste it I decided to wear it myself.'

'Well, you've got the figure for it, hasn't she, Simon?'

Her cheeks burned as she felt Simon's eyes assess the soft curves concealed by the gold silk. When he had finished she felt as though he knew every inch of her body intimately; as though nothing had been concealed from him.

'So when is the big day?' Alison demanded a little later. 'Mel and I were talking about it only last week. What a pity the boys aren't girls, then they could be bridesmaids. You are having a church ceremony, aren't you? I do think they're lovely. So much more of a sense of occasion about them than a register office ceremony. Hasn't Simon got you a ring yet?' She frowned as she noticed India's bare left hand, and looked reproachfully at her cousin. 'Oh, Simon!'

'I can't make up my mind what would suit her best,' Simon replied.

'Oh, but surely an emerald, to match her eyes. Your mother had one, I remember, it was . . .' Her voice faltered away as she looked into Simon's shuttered face. 'Oh dear,' she said helplessly. 'I'm sorry, Simon. Look, I think you'd better take me back to the hotel. I promised Mel I'd ring him before I go to bed. I don't know what happened when he was away for those few days, but ever since he returned he's been so considerate and sweet that I can hardly believe he's the same man who could only spare us the odd half hour from business not three months ago . . .'

She looked as though she were about to say more, but Simon stopped her, calling for the bill.

'Take me back first,' Alison instructed Simon as they left the restaurant. 'I'm sure you want some time to yourselves. I haven't forgotten what it feels like to be newly engaged and very much in love!' she chuckled. 'I knew it must be love the morning we arrived so inopportunely at the house; never before in my life have I caught my cool cousin out in such a compromising situation!' When India flushed, she said remorsefully, 'Oh, that tongue of mine! I didn't mean what you thought, India; I was simply trying to say that I've never known Simon to be so involved with anyone before as to behave so uncircumspectly. He's normally very careful about keeping his private life extremely private.'

'A mistake I'm going to have to pay dearly for,' Simon said tersely, drawing a puzzled look from his cousin.

Alison was staying at the Savoy. Simon went inside with her while India waited in the car.

'There's no need to run me home,' she told him when he returned. 'I'll get a taxi.'

Her comment was greeted with silence and then the powerful roar of the engine as her words were ignored and the car was set in motion.

With the streets illuminated only by sporadic street lights it was some time before India realised that they were travelling in the opposite direction from her flat.

'I hope you aren't planning on kidnapping me again,' she announced in what she hoped was a relatively assured voice. For some reason the silence in the car had taken on a thick tension which stiffened her muscles in an automatic reflex action. Her head felt muzzy from the wine she had drunk—far more than she normally consumed—and waves of sleep kept washing over her.

'Hardly after the results of my first attempt,' came the bitter response. 'I want to talk to you—to see if we can find a way to resolve this whole mess.'

He braked as he spoke driving into an underground garage, and parking the car.

India clambered reluctantly from its warmth when he opened the door, the cold air making her shiver violently, and also reacting badly with the wine she had drunk. Although mentally she felt quite calm and in control her legs for some reason seemed unable to obey the commands of her brain. Nevertheless she managed to follow Simon to the lift, which whisked them upwards before depositing them outside the penthouse suite of the block.

The interior of his apartment came as a surprise. Far from being the cold, clinical place she had visualised, the large drawing room was comfortably furnished, if somewhat masculine, with supple leather chesterfields and several excellent pieces of good antiques, including a delightful Regency table.

'Sit down,' he commanded, sliding her coat from her shoulders. When she shivered he touched a switch illuminating an electric fire which immediately began to heat the room. The effect of its dancing flames was almost hypnotic and India closed her eyes, aware of Simon moving about behind her.

'Drink this.'

It was on the tip of her tongue to tell him that she had already had more than enough to drink, but her fingers were already closing round the stem of the brandy balloon, and somehow she found herself obediently tilting the glass to her lips at his command, the fiery liquid burning its way down her throat.

'So . . . let's talk, shall we? How much is it going to cost me to get out of this engagement—quietly and quickly?'

India knew that her mouth must have fallen open. Perhaps it had been stupid of her, but when Simon had said he wanted to talk she had never dreamed that he actually imagined that he could buy her off, like . . . like someone he had simply bought for the night!

A combination of anger and alcohol overrode the caution warning her that he was in a dangerous mood, and she turned on him, indignation in every line of her tense body. 'I don't believe I'm hearing this! You can't honestly believe . . .'

'What I believe,' he said tersely, cutting across her, 'is that you deliberately provoked this situation. Like I said, without Mel to finance you, you need another backer. At first I thought the whole thing was simply a naïve attempt to force me into marriage, but then I realised that I wasn't giving you full credit for subtlety; that what you really wanted was to force me to pay you off.'

'Pay me off? Why, you . . . You couldn't!' she told him fiercely. 'And do you know why? Because despite your wealth, Simon Herries, I won't be bought!'

'No? Then what do you call the money you had from Mel?' he demanded thickly. 'God, if I have to endure this farce, I might as well get what I can from it!' He reached for her before she could move, his arms like iron bands as they imprisoned her, his mouth savagely punishing as it plundered the soft-ness of her parted lips.

She tried to push him away, but his weight was forcing her farther down into the chesterfield, one arm clamping her to him while the other found the zipper of her dress and slid it expertly down.

Beneath it she was wearing only her stockings and the smallest of briefs, and she clutched at the gold silk desperately as she felt the cool air against her back, but she was no match for Simon Herries. His hard fingers found the softness of her breast, the inti-mate contact making her release her dress auto-matically as she tried to avoid the physical contact of his flesh against hers. The opportunity was turned to good use, his muttered, 'Any more of that and I'll rip the damned thing apart!' making her freeze with fear as well as anger.

'That's better,' he grunted softly when she lay motionless in his arms. 'After all, it isn't as though this was the first time you've had to pay for your supper, I'm quite sure . . . Alison told me that you worked in Paris for a time with one of the top coutu-riers. Jobs like that are as scarce as hen's teeth. What did you do? Sleep with him?'

'Would you believe that I had talent?' India gritted back.

'Most assuredly, but at what? Not designing, I'll bet. Well, let's just see how your "talent" measures up, shall we?'

Later India was unable to believe that what did happen had. She knew when Simon removed her dress, because she shivered suddenly, trying desper-ately to conceal from him the pale thrust of her breasts, but he simply laughed, forcing her arms down at her sides and levering himself upwards, examining her body as callously as he might have done a piece of furniture he was thinking of buying.

'Nice,' he commented, his fingertips tracing the curve of her breast. His thumb had found her nipple and was stroking it softly.

Against her will India felt her body react. To her horror the sensitive flesh peaked and hardened, swelling beneath his expert arousal. Alternate waves of heat and anguish washed over her. She had never been in such a situation before, never allowed herself to get close enough to anyone to indulge in such intimacies, and it was too late now to regret her lack of experience, to wonder at her body's treacherous response; the hot, melting sensations flooding through her, and the unbelievable urge welling up inside her to reach for the dark head and bring those firm male lips to the flesh his thumb was tormenting.

She shuddered with self-revulsion. What was happening to her? Had the natural desires she had denied for so long suddenly turned traitor on her? She moaned pleadingly as Simon's mouth grazed the tender skin of her throat, finding the sensitive hollows behind her ears, tormenting her cheeks and eyelids.

'I'll give you ten out of ten for desirability,' he muttered thickly at one point, his lips against her ear. 'But you don't rate very highly on reciprocation. Surely a woman like you doesn't need to be told what a man likes? You've got beautiful breasts,' he added seconds later, his mouth no longer against her ear, but fulfilling her earlier wish as he explored first the shadowy cleft between them and then the taut fullness of her breasts themselves, the sensuous rasp of his tongue sending her almost mindless with a pleasure which far exceeded anything she had ever even imagined existed.

She didn't even realise that she was clinging mindlessly to his shoulders until he lifted his head to mutter hoarsely. 'For God's sake don't tease—take this damned shirt off for me and let me feel you against me . . .'

Scarcely aware of what she was doing, India moved like a sleepwalker, her fingers moving softly over the buttons of his shirt, her mouth dry with tension as she stared up at the tanned smoothness of his body etched with deeper shadows where his body hair covered the taut muscles. A faint sheen of sweat gleamed across his chest, the musky, indefinably exciting odour filling her nostrils, some inner compulsion forcing her to place lips which trembled nervously against the damp flesh.

She heard Simon groan, burying his head against her. His hands explored the trembling contours of her body, triggering off waves of sensuous pleasure, reactions she had never dreamed herself capable of, so that when Simon at last unfastened the belt of his trousers, removing the last of her own clothes at the same time, she was able to make no demure.

The abrasive touch of his body hair against the soft fullness of her breasts was erotically pleasurable, her fingers discovering and exploring the sleek muscles of his back, her lips travelling shyly over his skin.

She gasped in mingled shock and pleasure when his hand stroked urgently along her thighs, arousing a tide of emotions which completely obliterated the last remnants of her ability to reason.

'If you react like this to all your lovers, no wonder they come back for more,' he told her jerkily, making no secret of his own arousal, his lips teasing brief kisses over her stomach and lower until she was almost delirious with pleasure.

When Simon parted her thighs and she felt the full potently male weight of him, the urgent thrust of a desire that excited and aroused her she felt no fear—a fact for which she was later to blame the large glass of brandy on top of too much wine—in fact she was as eager for his possession as he was to possess her, her body trembling achingly, her mouth parting in tremulous desire.

The sharp, unexpected pain was the first intrusion of reality. She tensed automatically, but it was too late by far for going back.

In awful silence she felt Simon freeze before he moved away from her, reaching for his clothes. He was sitting on the chesterfield with his back to her. He passed her her dress which she surveyed with acute distaste, unable to believe that she had actually allowed—no, not allowed, her mind forced her to acknowledge, but actively encouraged him to . . . To make love to her, a cool little voice said acidly. She had allowed Simon Herries to possess her.

Simon still had his back to her. When he did speak his voice was taut with reined-in anger and something else India could not distinguish.

'A virgin!' he almost spat out the words as though he hated the taste of them. 'How come?' he demanded sharply. 'No, don't tell me—you were holding out for the highest bidder, was that it?'

For a moment she was too hurt to speak, but then she found her voice.

'You are quite wrong,' she told him, trying not to let her voice tremble. 'I was waiting until I met the man I could love enough to make it a worthwhile experience—the sort of experience it should be, not some cheap shoddy affair, quickly over and quickly forgotten. What I didn't bargain for was meeting a man who prejudged me, walked all over me with hobnailed boots and then decided to "make love" to me simply because he thought I owed it to him. Because he thought I was a liar and a cheat, even though I'd told him that it simply wasn't true.'

'Why didn't you tell me you were a virgin?'

'Why should I? What possible business could it have been of yours?'

'I should have thought that was self-evident,' he told India curtly. 'Why the hell didn't you tell me that you weren't having an affair with Mel?'

'I tried to—remember?'

'But he wanted to have an affair with you?' he persisted.

India nodded her head. 'He . . . that is, he . . . he wanted . . .!

'I think we may safely take his desires as read,' Simon responded dryly. 'What I'm interested in right at this moment are yours.'

There was nothing to be gained from concealing the truth now, India decided tiredly.

'I like Mel,' she said slowly, 'and I valued his friendship—but he hasn't given me any financial assistance, as you said, and it was true that I didn't get in touch with the papers . . .'

'But you don't love Mel?'

India shook her head, her voice thick with bitter self-loathing as she said, 'If I did do you think for one moment that I'd have . . . that tonight . . .'

'We're all human,' came the surprisingly compassionate response. 'It isn't exactly unusual for a woman to turn from a man she can't have to one she can. So, you don't love Mel, and there's no one else in your life?'

Not sure where his questions were leading, India shook her head numbly. Now that it was over she found it hard to understand how she had behaved as she had; how she had reacted so passionately to Simon Herries when other men . . .

'I think I'd better go now,' she said awkwardly. 'I'll—I'll leave it to you to break the news of the termination of our engagement to your grandmother and Alison . . .'

There could be no question now of him holding her by threats to their bogus engagement. India suspected that, like her, he would probably be only too glad for their association to end.

'We're in agreement on one point,' Simon told her grimly. 'Our engagement will certainly have to be terminated.'

It was her own suggestion after all; so why should she feel this acute sense of loss, this agonising despair?

'I'll see about a marriage licence in the morning.'

India stared at him, her body stiffening defensively. 'A marriage licence? But. . . .'

Simon had his back to her, but he turned to look at her pale face, his expression unreadable as he told her, 'You do realise that you're being less than flattering?' His mouth twisted wryly. 'I am after all merely doing the time-honoured thing—gentleman seduces innocent virgin unwittingly and then marries her. Isn't it the very stuff of romance?'

'But there's no need ... I mean ...'

'I know what you mean, but contrary to your naïve faith and optimism, there could well be every need. I am referring to the fact that you could have conceived my child. You must forgive me for sounding ridiculously sentimental, but I have a peculiar disinclination to see the life I might have created destroyed on the operating table.'

In spite of herself India felt a curious lump rise in her throat, an aching pain that spread through her body.

'But you can't know,' she protested in a shaky whisper. 'I might not. . . .'

'We can't afford to take the chance,' Simon told her firmly. 'You've already admitted there's no one else in your life—the situation may not be ideal, but we're in no worse a position than partners in an arranged marriage.'

'And if it turns out that I'm not ... not ...'

'Carrying my child?' Simon supplied. 'In that case, after a suitable interval we can have the marriage annulled.' He looked at her. 'You needn't fear that because of what's happened tonight I intend to demand my rights as your "husband".'

Meaning what? India wondered bitterly. That he would continue to take his pleasure with the sophisticated women he normally chose as his companions?

As though he had read her mind he added harshly, 'Neither shall I embarrass you with liaisons of the sort which the gutter press seem to delight in. In return I ask only that you give our union a chance, for the sake of our child ...'

'There may not be one,' India protested, but she was weakening and she knew it. It was all very well for Simon to talk of an abortion, but she knew herself well enough to know that she could never destroy a life growing within her, and while she was financially secure enough to provide for her child no amount of material possessions could replace a united family unit; the presence of a father in a child's life ... It wouldn't be easy. And yet, as Simon had said, they were no worse off than the participants in an arranged marriage.

'Well?' Simon demanded, frowning suddenly as he saw her face. 'For God's sake, why did you let me think ...'

'That I was an experienced woman of the world? You didn't leave me much choice.'

'I'm sorry that I hurt you,' he said tersely. 'If I'd known ...'

'It wasn't intentional ... I should have stopped you ... Now, I'd like to go home,' she added, 'There's an awful lot to think about.'

'I'll take you.'

He drove her home in silence, saying as he escorted her to her door, 'I'll be in touch later on. Don't do anything foolish, will you, India?'

She shook her head, half blinded by the tears which had suddenly filled her eyes. A terrible sense of desolation swept over her as she watched him leave. Had she really agreed to marry him; a man who not twenty-four hours before she had considered her worst enemy? And why? For the sake of a child she might not even have conceived!

Alone in her flat she found herself reliving those moments in Simon's arms—the intense arousal of her senses; her passionate response to him, her willingness to fall in with his plans. And then she admitted the truth. She had fallen in love with him!

Once the truth was acknowledged so much that had puzzled her fell into place—her intense awareness of him; the driving force of the anger she had kept lashing into heated fury to prevent herself from recognising the truth, the capitulation of her body at his first touch. She loved him! What on earth was she going to do? She couldn't possibly marry him now! But did she have any choice? While he thought there was the slightest possibility that she might have conceived his child he would never allow her to escape him. And did she really want to? Who knew, perhaps within the framework of their marriage affection, if not love, might come. But would it be enough? Something pagan deep inside her said 'no'. She wanted his love; a love that matched her own.

At last, after what seemed to be hours of hard arguing backwards and forwards, she gave in to the clamourings of her heart. If fate had decreed that Simon should offer her marriage who was she to refuse? Let what must be be. Perhaps it was cowardly of her, but she lacked the strength and determination to fight both her love and Simon.

CHAPTER SEVEN

THEY were married a week later in the same small village church where Simon's parents had been married, and during the brief ceremony India caught herself praying that their marriage would prove more secure and enduring. Which was extremely foolish of her, she told herself afterwards sipping champagne and trying not to look as bemused as she felt as Simon introduced her to various people, because if any marriage was doomed to failure theirs surely must be. She didn't doubt Simon's good intentions, but how long would it be before he found himself longing for the sophistication of women such as Ursula and Melisande?

It was something India tried not to think about. Alison had been both delighted and horrified when Simon informed her how quickly they were to be married, and despite her pregnancy had insisted that the simple no-fuss ceremony Simon was planning was unfair to India, who would want to cherish the memory of her wedding day.

Instead, Alison had organised a small, informal buffet party at her house, and although India was touched by her thoughtfulness in many ways she would have preferred just herself, Simon and the necessary witnesses. There was something bordering on the temptation of bad luck about celebrating what was no more than a formal business arrangement in such a way.

Simon had asked India what she preferred to do after their marriage; if she wished to move into his flat which had a spare bedroom, or if she would prefer them to start afresh. If there was to be a child, he had pointed out, the flat would hardly be suitable, for all its luxury.

Moved by an impulse she could barely comprehend, India had asked if it would not be possible for them to move down to the cottage, regretting the words the moment they were spoken, as she saw Simon frown and hesitate.

'So you managed it after all!'

She hadn't seen Ursula Blanchard approaching her. The older woman's eyes raked the plain cream silk dress and jacket India had chosen for the ceremony—not her own design as there had not been time to make anything suitable but an outfit she had bought from Bellville Sassoon and which bore their unmistakable stamp.

'You're not wearing white, I notice,' Ursula murmured cattily. 'Very wise of you, my dear—no one knowing Simon would have believed you had the right ... Oh, there you are, darling,' she cooed as Simon, tall, and unbelievably handsome in a dark formal suit and crisp silk shirt, came towards them. 'I was just telling your little bride how fortunate she was.' Her fingers stroked the fabric of Simon's suit, and India felt nausea rise up inside her as she pictured those plum-tipped nails digging passionately into tanned male flesh; the sullen, pouting lips, parting beneath the skilled insistence of Simon's ... She moved blindly away, appalled by the depth of her emotions; the strength of her jealousy, her face paling suddenly, causing Simon to frown and glance at her from beneath hooded lids. As she turned away India caught Ursula's deliberately outstretched arm, and a full glass of champagne cascaded over the cream silk.

'Oh dear!' the other woman exclaimed insincerely, 'You must send me the cleaners' bill—or perhaps the bill for your outfit, it might be cheaper. Was it one of your own designs?'

India gaped at her effrontery, convinced that somehow Ursula had deliberately stepped forward as she moved, and spilt her drink. Simon was looking away, his expression withdrawn, and India flushed, fearing that he might think she was given to snide exchanges of the sort Ursula had promoted.

'I ought to be getting changed anyway,' she said quietly. 'If you'll both excuse me.'

'Take all the time you like. I'll see to it that Simon doesn't get bored. I'm good at that, aren't I, darling?'

Feeling sicker by the minute, India managed to walk away with commendable poise, but her self-control deserted her the minute she reached the room Alison had set aside for her to change in, and she was sitting staring out of the window, making no attempt to do anything about her damp dress, when Alison walked in.

'Are you all right?' the other woman asked anxiously. 'I saw Ursula collaring Simon.' She pulled a wry face. 'Dreadful creature! You mustn't let her get you down. She really must have the hide of an ox—Simon has been trying to shake her off for ages, but she simply won't take the hint.'

'He didn't seem to be doing much shaking off just now,' India commented in what she had intended to be a light tone, but which instead sounded more than a little shaky.

Alison took her hand. 'Poor India! She is rather a man-eater, isn't she? But you really mustn't worry. It's obvious how Simon feels about you.'

If only Alison knew! India found herself thinking grimly as the older woman sat down. Her face and ankles were slightly puffy despite the fact that her pregnancy was only in the sixth month, and watching her India could not help remembering what Mel had said about his wife's state of health.

'You shouldn't have done all this,' she felt moved to say to Alison. 'You look dreadfully tired.'

'I'm fine, and besides, I enjoyed it. Left to himself Simon would have got married in a dreadful hole-and-corner fashion. My only regret is that neither of his parents were alive to see today. Have you decided where you're going to live yet?' she added, changing the subject. 'Rather selfishly I can't help hoping you might decide to move down here. I know most of the structural work on the house is finished, but I suppose you'll want to keep the London flat on for the sake of your work.'

'We haven't really had time to discuss it yet,' India told her truthfully. Whenever she had thought about the future and her possible marriage, before meeting Simon she had always visualised herself continuing to design, possibly even when the children arrived, although not at the salon as she did now, but in her own home. Jenny was more than capable of running the salon side of the business. She had worked very hard and India would have liked to reward her in this way, but she was a little reluctant to make any firm plans until she had spoken to Simon. The fact had to be faced that he might not want her in the home he had once shared with his parents; that he might prefer to keep their relationship to the sterile atmosphere of the London flat. She hadn't forgotten his reaction when she had first raised the subject of them living at the cottage.

The final goodbyes had been said; India had received an affectionate kiss from Simon's grandmother, who despite her wry smile had had tears in her eyes as she gathered with the other guests to wave them off.

They didn't have time for a proper honeymoon, Simon had told her when she had enquired where he intended taking India, but India knew that the real reason must be that he didn't really want to be alone with her, and more than ever she wished she had not allowed herself to be carried along on the crest of an emotional wave into a marriage which she grew more convinced with every passing second was doomed to fail.

There was the usual confetti and trail of tin cans adorning the Ferrari—although the sleek car had escaped the indignity of slogans painted all over it in shaving foam; his nephews probably weren't yet aware of the handiness of such a weapon, Simon had commented when he stopped on a quiet side road discreetly out of sight of the guests, and got out to remove the offending articles.

Glad of an opportunity to break the stifling silence which had seemed to fill the interior of the car the moment they left the reception, India said eagerly that they seemed very pleasant boys.

'They are—Mel's a lucky man both in his wife and his children.'

'He is,' India agreed warmly. 'Alison is a lovely person.' Her face clouded as she remembered the other woman's tired face. 'I'm only worried that the work of giving us such a lovely reception might have proved too much for her in her present condition. Did you notice how tired she looked?'

She was startled when Simon stopped the car, resting his forearms on the wheel as he turned to look at her, an expression she could not define in his eyes.

'You're one real nice lady, Mrs Simon Herries,' he told her with an exaggerated transatlantic drawl. 'Do you know that? And while we're on the subject it seems that I owe you yet another apology. Ursula and I had a most interesting discussion while you were upstairs repairing the damage caused by that glass of champagne she slung over you. Did you know that she was the one who told the Press about us?'

'I suspected,' India confessed. 'In fact I tried to tell you in the car that time, but you made me so furious that I couldn't get through to you.'

Something about the way Simon was regarding her was making her pulses race, her heart thumping unsteadily as she tried not to let her own eyes drop. A ridiculous shyness washed over her, and she didn't realise that she was fidgeting nervously with her seat-belt, until firm warm fingers closed over her own, uncurling them from the strip of fabric, and lifting them to lips that for the first time since she had known their owner seemed to be curling upwards in a smile. And what a smile! Her heart lurched and then suddenly started beating erratically, as she stared upwards as mesmerised as a small rabbit caught in the powerful glare of the Ferrari's head-lights.

'You know,' Simon commented conversationally, 'if I didn't know you better I'd think you were nervous. What of?' he asked her unexpectedly. 'That I'll go back on my promise and claim the rights this——' he touched the plain gold band adorning her finger beneath the magnificent square-cut emerald engagement ring he had given her—'gives me?'

'Oh no, I'm sure you wouldn't ... wh-what I mean ... I'm sure you'd never go back on your word,' she managed huskily in the end.

'Umm. Which leaves me in something of a quandary, doesn't it? Either I prove that I'm a rogue whose word means nothing, or I run the risk of having my very attractive wife turn to someone else for consolation following the neglect of her husband.'

India couldn't understand him in this changed mood, and her eyes, green mirrors of bewilderment, showed her bemusement.

'Shall we try and start again?' Simon suggested softly. 'We're married now—for better, for worse—let's try and make it for better. Not perhaps straight away. I'm prepared to give you time to get used to me, but,' he smiled again, this time teasingly, 'we both know that we aren't indifferent to one another, eh? You see, India, my own parents were divorced, and because of the misery I suffered, I've always sworn that I'd never inflict on any child of mine the trauma I experienced. It's a terrible thing for a child to be torn between its parents.'

'I know,' India agreed in a low voice. 'I feel the same way.'

'There you are! We're both in agreement, and I believe that with a lot of goodwill and patience we can make this marriage work . . .'

'For the sake of the baby I might be carrying?' India asked slowly, not knowing quite why she felt impelled to differentiate between the situation should she be pregnant and the situation should they discover that she was not after all.

'Yes. Well, do we have a bargain? A vow from us both to join the other vows we've already made today, but this time a private one. A vow that we'll both try to make this marriage work. When I made love to you . . .' he seemed to hesitate as though choosing his words with care, 'although it sounds facile now to say so, had I known that you were a virgin, that you'd never known a man . . .'

'You wouldn't have made love to me?' India supplied, forcing a shaky smile 'I kn . . .'

'I'm a man, India, not a saint,' Simon corrected her with a wry smile. 'No, what I was going to say was that I would have ensured that the experience was not as . . . traumatic as it was.'

India looked away, trying to conceal from him the unexpected tears welling in her eyes. Did that mean that he had desired her? That it hadn't simply been anger that had prompted his actions?

'I . . .' She tried to speak and then shook her head when the words refused to come. Simon's hand was warm against her chin as he tilted her face upwards.

'I hurt you—you cried out. Unavoidable perhaps, but I could have been less . . . brutal, for the lack of another word. I don't want you to think that what you experienced in my arms on that occasion is the sum total of how it feels to make love. You're a passionate little thing,' he added slowly. 'Surprisingly so when one considers all that cool control you consistently assume. So,' he said briskly, changing the subject, 'shall we make that vow?'

Suddenly shy, India could only nod her head, her eyes widening with shock as Simon bent his head, his intention unmistakably clear as his hand slid from her jaw to the back of her head, to tangle in her hair, and secure her against the warmth of his own body as he kissed her; lightly at first, on the eyelids and forehead, before slowly parting her lips with the tip of his tongue, his breath fanning slightly across her skin.

'You can kiss me back, you know,' he whispered teasingly in her ear, when she made no attempt to respond, holding herself rigidly in check too terrified to betray how she felt about him to risk the response she knew she would give once she allowed her emotions to get out of hand. 'In fact you have to. It's a part of the bargain.'

'I . . .' Her voice sounded rusty and unfamiliar even to herself, and she was steeling herself to make some response when the sudden strident blare of a car horn caused Simon to swear and push her gently back into her own seat.

'Perhaps here is neither the time nor the place.' He glanced at his watch. 'We ought to be leaving anyway. There's something I want to show you.'

They drove for several miles through gentle rolling countryside, with Simon pointing out various landmarks to India. He was extremely knowledgeable about the countryside, and India would never have believed that she could be so relaxed in his company.

'Here we are,' he exclaimed at last, turning off the main road and in through tall wrought iron gates, set either side of a gravel drive, lawns and shrubs stretching away at either side, the rhododendrons a vivid splash of colour with their pinks, lilacs and mauve flowers. 'Before the Boer War a fine avenue of elms marched either side of this drive,' he told her. 'They were planted by the first Herries to own Meadow's End. He bought it in the 1800s with the money he made from sugar plantations and slavery. There's a painting of the avenue in the library. The trees were cut down during the Boer War for ships.'

'You mean *this* is Meadow's End—your home?' India demanded, almost breathless with awe. 'I never dreamed. . . Alison told me . . .'

'Oh, it isn't nearly so impressive as it seems. Part of the house was bombed during the last war—the Victorian wing, fortunately, a hideous monstrosity, and then the people who bought it from my father went bankrupt, just about the time when large old houses were at a low premium and everyone wanted a modern split-level with all mod cons, so it fell into complete disrepair. It hasn't been easy getting it restored. The shell that was left was Queen Anne and I've had a devil of a job finding men to restore it as it was. It's been easier these last few years since there's been a revival of interest in older houses.'

They turned a corner in the drive, and Simon stopped the car. India didn't need to ask why. Although they hadn't quite reached it, before them lay the house, graceful and perfectly symmetrical two large sash windows either side of the main door on the ground floor, two more above those and then smaller, dormer replicas let into the roof.

The late afternoon sun caught the house in its dying glow, deepening the mellow red brick to russet, and picking out the stone above the front door with the date carved deeply into it.

A country gentleman, Alison had said, but she had never dreamed she had meant something like this!

'It's beautiful,' she said simply to Simon, and as though no other words were necessary, he started the car and drove, not to the front of the house, but round the back into what had obviously been a stable yard, but what was now garaging with what looked like a mews flat above.

'The house is empty,' Simon warned India as he opened her door for her. 'It's only just been finished—it isn't even decorated yet.'

'It's lovely,' India repeated, thinking wistfully of how much she would enjoy transforming the bare, echoing rooms Simon was showing her into what they could be.

'Drawing room,' he told her briefly, opening the door on to a large rectangular room with windows overlooking the front and the side of the house.

They had come in via the back door, into a large but empty room which he told her had been a small parlour, but which was now intended to be the kitchen. There was also a large dining room; a library complete with shelved walls, as yet empty of books, and a generously proportioned but not intimidating room which India immediately visualised as a comfortable family room.

The hall was square, with a black and white tiled floor, and an intricately carved staircase curving upwards to a galleried landing.

India ran her fingers lightly over the carving, delighting in the smooth rich feel of the wood beneath her fingers.

'At one time most of the downstairs rooms were panelled in linenfold,' Simon told her, 'but a modern-thinking Regency Herries had it all ripped out and replaced it with the Adams-style décor you can see now. Fortunately, however, money ran out before he got to the staircase, which was carved by Grinling Gibbons. Do you think you could settle happily here?'

India was astounded.

'Happily?' She blinked and looked up uncertainly, not sure she had heard him correctly. 'Who couldn't?' she managed to say when she had got her breath back.

'Plenty of women,' Simon assured her. 'You'd be surprised. Ursula, for instance, hated this place. She prefers my London flat. Of course, there's a tremendous amount of work to be done yet. I'm thinking of getting in a firm of interior designers. I have a few pieces of good furniture—things that my aunt and uncle managed to salvage from here for me, and which Alison has kindly given house room to . . .'

'I could do it,' India offered impulsively. 'That is . . . I would love to do it, if you trust me.'

'I trust you. With my home *and* my cheque book!'

For some reason the dry words brought a lump to India's throat. She was getting far too emotional, she told herself; letting all manner of foolish romantic notions take hold of her.

'I thought we'd spend tonight at the cottage,' Simon told her. 'It's only three miles away. I have to go to London tomorrow. You know that I have extensive business interests—some in television; one being the series Melisande is to appear in. Well, it just so happens that the Americans are considering buying the series. If the deal goes through it will assure South-Mid's success, so tomorrow's meeting is quite important.'

On the drive back to the cottage, Simon was silent, and rather than intrude upon his thoughts India kept quiet too.

The cottage was warm when they stepped inside. In the living room someone had laid a fire, and while Simon bent to set a match to it India wandered into the kitchen. There was a note propped up against the kettle, which said simply 'Wine and food in fridge, if you need them—God bless, Alison.'

'Are you hungry?' she asked Simon, who was kneeling in front of the fire coaxing it into life. 'Alison had left us steak and plenty of fresh salad.'

'Umm. I seem to remember you're quite a good cook.' He laughed as she blushed, but it wasn't unkind laughter.

It was a curiously domestic scene; Simon lighting the fire and then coming in the the kitchen to take cutlery from the drawer while India busied herself with the steak and the preparation of a mixed salad. She was just finishing the dressing when Simon wandered back from the living room and came over to watch her, leaning against the table, his arms folded.

'I thought we'd eat in the living room, and then have an early night.'

Mingled excitement and alarm coiled through India's stomach.

'If that's what you want. Could you take the salad

through?' She was trying to sound calm. 'The steak's nearly ready.'

'You can certainly cook,' Simon pronounced fifteen minutes later, cutting into his steak. 'Clever girl!'

He poured them both a second glass of wine. India, who had barely touched any food at the reception, could feel it going to her head. Her appetite was almost non-existent, her body so tense that she jumped visibly when Simon knocked a spoon to the floor. Aware of his eyes upon her, India kept hers on her plate, wishing that her heart wouldn't race so nervously. She was aware of Simon as she had never been aware of any man before; the way his mouth quirked downwards before he smiled; the hard chiselled lines of lips she felt an insane longing to touch with her fingers; the strong column of his throat rising from the cream silk shirt, which he had opened at the neck when he lit the fire; the lean tapering fingers which, if she closed her eyes, she could almost feel against her breast, cupping and moulding . . .

'India?' She jumped guiltily. 'You were miles away—where?'

'Nowhere.'

'Mmm, hardly flattering for a newly married woman. Come here,' he commanded softly, rising from his chair and coming towards her.

Like someone in a dream India rose slowly from her seat, her eyes fixed blindly on Simon's. His fingers circled her wrists, stroking the soft inner flesh gently, and sending her pulses racing.

'I haven't forgotten the little matter of a kiss you owe me,' Simon whispered, his mouth teasing feather-light kisses against her throat, where he had pushed back the weight of her hair to reveal the pale creamy skin, and allow his warm lips access to the vulnerable curve of her neck.

'Well?' he murmured, nuzzling the soft skin behind her ear, his teeth nipping the lobe sharply when she didn't reply. His hands, which had been on her waist, moved upwards, one arm curving her towards him while the other pushed aside the flimsy silk blouse she was wearing to reveal the silk camisole top beneath, finding the tender point of her breast with unerring ease, and teasing it into peaking pleasure beneath the frail fabric.

'Beautiful,' he murmured throatily, as he slid aside her blouse and camisole to reveal the pale flesh with its pink aureole.

As his dark head bent towards her breast India felt her heart beat slow to thudding, painful strokes, her breath locked tightly in her throat.

When Simon swung her up in his arms and carried her to the rug in front of the fire, she made no demur as he slowly undressed her, studying the tender curves of her breasts in the firelight before anointing each one with kisses that sent desire spiralling dizzily inside her, making her arch instinctively and lock her hands behind his neck.

'India . . .'

The sharp ring of the telephone shattered across the intimacy of their surroundings, making India stiffen and Simon groan.

'I suppose I'd better answer it, but if it's one of my nephews playing a practical joke I'll give them both such sore backsides that they won't sit down for a week! Don't go away, will you?' he asked softly with a smile, dropping a soft light kiss on her half opened mouth before disappearing into the hall.

He was gone quite a long time. Long enough for India to start to feel foolish and cold without her clothes, and she was pulling on her camisole top when he walked back in.

'Bad news, I'm afraid,' he told her briefly. 'That American deal I was telling you about has suddenly developed a problem, and I'm going to have to leave for London right away.'

'At this time of night?' India protested, flushing as she realised that she sounded like a nagging wife.

'To us it's night,' Simon said dryly. 'To our trans-atlantic cousins it's the middle of the day. I don't know when I'll be back. Will you be okay? I could ring Alison.'

'No, I'll be fine on my own,' India told him hastily. 'I'll sleep in the room I had before. I . . .'

'The bed isn't made up,' Simon told her tersely. 'India, I'm sorry about this, but it can't be avoided. Don't forget our vow while I'm gone, will you?'

'I won't,' India told him in a low voice.

'Good girl! I'm not going to kiss you goodbye—I daren't. If I did I'd never be able to walk out of here.'

Very flattering of him, but scarcely true, India reflected several minutes later when the Ferrari's throaty roar had died away and she was alone. She couldn't deceive herself that she was anywhere as near as desirable as the other women Simon had known. And yet he had desired her. Her heart warmed as she remembered the way he had looked at her before the phone rang. He had as good as said that he wanted their marriage to be normal; that he wanted her in his bed as well as in his home. Her depression started to lift. When he returned they would be able to make a fresh start, she promised herself; she would concentrate on all that was promising in their relationship and ignore its flaws. Every relationship possessed some flaws.

It was in a mood of optimism that she prepared for bed, discarding the fine crêpe-de-chine nightdress she had put in her case in favour of the warmth of the pyjama jacket she had found on the bed, washed and ironed.

There was a certain amount of sensual pleasure to be found in lying in Simon's bed, in imagining his body next to hers, but no amount of imagining was any substitute for the real thing, she thought ruefully as her tense muscles refused to relax, and her body ached for the appeasement Simon's possession would have brought.

But there was always tomorrow, she told herself; a whole host of tomorrows—and on that infinitely pleasurable thought she fell asleep.

CHAPTER EIGHT

THE telephone ringing woke her. At first she couldn't remember where she was, and then when she did, she dashed downstairs, thinking the caller would be Simon.

The intensity of her disappointment when she realised it wasn't was a barometer of her love for him, had she needed one, and it was several seconds before she realised that Alison, far from sounding her usual calm self, sounded distinctly worried.

'You say Simon isn't there?'

'I'm afraid not,' said India. 'He had to dash off to London. A meeting with some important Americans. Is there anything I can do?'

'Do you really mean that, or are you just being polite?'

'I really mean it,' India assured her firmly. 'What's the problem?'

'I'm probably being silly—after all, I've had two children already—but this morning when I woke up I felt a bit off, and with Mel being away . . . Well, to be honest with you I was going to ask if you and Simon would care to come over for lunch. Dreadful of me, I know, when you're supposed to be on your honeymoon, but . . .'

'Well, Simon isn't here, but if I will do I'd love to come over,' India assured her. 'In fact I'd be glad of the company.' She had intended to spend the morning on some initial outline plans for the house, but the faint shakiness in Alison's voice alarmed her. 'I'll ring for a taxi and be with you just as soon as I can be.'

Giving her the address and apologising again for imposing on her, Alison rang off, leaving India distinctly alarmed. She rang the number of a taxi firm she found in the yellow pages and within an hour of Alison's call she was on her way to the house.

Quite what she had expected to find she wasn't sure, but it certainly wasn't Alison, perched on a small stepladder while she cleaned the kitchen windows.

'Oh, I'm feeling fine now,' Alison exclaimed gaily in reply to India's anxious query. 'In fact I haven't felt quite so well in weeks, so I decided to give these a clean while I was in the mood. I hope you don't mind quiche and salad for lunch?'

'I'd love it,' India assured her. 'Look, why don't you let me finish those while you have a rest?'

'They're nearly done, but if you really want to make yourself useful you could make us both a cup of coffee. What a shame Simon had to rush off to London like that. When did he go?'

When India told her she pulled a face. 'Oh, poor you—and poor Simon!' She grinned mischievously, suddenly looking much younger. 'I bet he wasn't in the least bit pleased. I detected unmistakable signs of a man impatient to have his bride to himself about my cousin yesterday—most out of character. I'm glad to see that cool calm ruffled for once,' she told India with satisfaction. 'You're a pretty cool one yourself. I've never seen a less emotional bride. Ursula Blanchard was furious, and so was I—with her! Fancy crashing the reception like that! How on earth she could be so brazen I'll never know, but then of course she always was pretty thick-skinned. She has an aunt living down here and when she got her hooks into Simon, every time he came down here so did she—and on the most flimsy of excuses. Poor darling, I think he was getting pretty fed up with her persistence, although he never said anything.'

'Oh, I don't think any man really minds being pursued by a beautiful woman,' India said lightly, hoping that she didn't betray herself, or her jealousy of Ursula Blanchard, whom Simon had after all at one time cared very deeply about.

'Beautiful and deadly,' Alison replied flippantly, giving the window a final wipe before stepping heavily down from the ladder while India steadied it for her. 'But Simon's far too wise a man to be caught in a man-trap. I remember once when I asked him about her he said that as a mistress she was ideal, but as a wife unthinkable.'

She said this with so much relish that India had to smile, but inwardly her heart ached and she had no difficulty whatsoever in envisaging in which category Simon placed her; good wife material, but inadequate as far as anything else went! She wasn't being fair to him or their marriage, she chided herself. Such negative thinking would get her nowhere. Simon himself had been the one to suggest that they wipe the slate clean; start off afresh and build a marriage which would endure as Alison's parents' had endured; but had she the courage to do that, knowing that she must always carry alone the burden of her love for him in the knowledge that on his side there would never be anything but acceptance and possibly affection?

Time alone would tell, she told herself, as she helped Alison to prepare their simple lunch.

'I hate the house when the boys have gone back to school,' Alison told her. They had both been allowed a day off school to attend the wedding and India knew that Mel had driven them back before flying up to Scotland on business.

'I'm glad you've married Simon,' Alison continued, deftly making French dressing. 'And not just for Simon's sake—for purely selfish reasons as well.' She turned to India, her brown eyes creased with pain. 'You see, with you married to Simon . . .' India's hand clenched on the knife she was holding poised above the quiche. Surely Alison didn't know

about her and Mel? Of course really there was
nothing to know, but India knew how she would
feel were she to discover that her husband had been
making overtures to another woman whether they
were reciprocated or not, and she could not bear for
Alison to be hurt unnecessarily. '. . . and Simon no
longer the eligible bachelor he was, I hope that Mel
will get over the envy he's always had of Simon.'
Her mouth twisted a little. 'Mel thinks I don't know
this, but I'm not totally blind. For the past year or
so he's been wallowing in what's commonly known
as early male menopause; yearning for his youth and
freedom, in other words. Oh, he's tried to hide it
from me, but I've seen the look on his face every
time he picks up a newspaper and sees Simon's
photograph there, and the ridiculous thing is that
really Mel isn't cut out to be a playboy. Still, I'm
hoping that Simon's marriage to you will make him
see that being a bachelor isn't all he thinks it is.
They say, don't they, that a baby never cements a
broken marriage. That's why I decided on this,' she
told India, patting her stomach. 'But it backfired.
Mel feels we're both too old to be starting another
baby, and the boys aren't too keen on the idea
either.' Her hands started to shake suddenly, tears
welling and rolling down her cheeks.

'Damn, damn!' she swore crossly. 'I didn't mean
to burden you with all this. I've already wept once
all over Simon, and I promised myself then that my
crying was done, but you see, I still love Mel just as
much as I did when we were first married, only now
instead of being an equal partner in our marriage I
feel that I'm excess baggage, a burden Mel has to
carry. Every time I see him looking at another

woman I'm eaten up with jealousy, wondering if she's the one who's going to take him from me.'

India put down the knife and went over to the figure bent over the mixing bowl.

'No one is going to take him from you,' she said firmly. 'Come and sit down. Now, Mel would be a fool to give up a wife like you for the chimera of middle-aged romance, and I'm sure he's sensible enough to realise that for himself. My mother once went through an experience similar to yours—worse, in fact, because there *was* another woman, but unlike wives today, she didn't give up, she hung on. It's only since I've grown up myself that I've realised what that must have cost her in terms of pride—and she was a very proud woman, and a very brave one, but in the end it was worth it—and I believe my father thought so too. Wait until the baby arrives,' she said softly. 'I'll bet Mel will be over the moon. After all, what better boost could there be to his ego, and you could always remind him that a baby in the house keeps its parents young.'

'I'll try and bear that in mind,' Alison laughed shakily, 'although if this one is anything like the other two, he'll make us both feel very, very old! Neither of them let us have a full night's sleep for two whole months.'

Glad that she had been able to divert Alison's thoughts, if only marginally, India gestured to the French dressing. 'That looks delicious, and I don't know about you, but I'm hungry!'

Nothing more was said about Mel over lunch, and India found herself saying a silent prayer for Alison's happiness. It was as they were drinking their coffee that she noticed Alison tense suddenly with pain, her face draining of colour.

'Indigestion,' she said with a laugh. 'Serves me right for being greedy and eating so much of that quiche.'

'It was delicious,' India agreed. 'Look, why don't you go upstairs and lie down for a little while? I'll see to everything down here, and then in an hour or so I'll make us both a drink.'

'You're spoiling me,' Alison protested, but India noticed that she was still tense, her face almost grey beneath her make-up, and alarm began to feather along her own nerve endings. Not wanting to alarm Alison, she said casually, 'Look, why don't I give your doctor a ring?'

'Why? Look, I'm six months pregnant, not nine, and besides, I've had enough experience to tell indigestion from labour pains. All the same, I think I will go and lie down for a while if you don't mind. The doctor did tell me I ought to try and rest.'

'So you start climbing ladders and cleaning windows,' India said dryly. 'I'll bring you a cup of tea up in an hour.'

It took her almost that to wash up, tidy the kitchen and glance through the paper she found on the pine dresser, and in all that time there was no sound from upstairs.

At three o'clock she brewed a pot of tea and poured a cup out for Alison, knocking gently on her bedroom door before opening it and tiptoeing in.

Alison wasn't asleep, but the moment she saw her, all thoughts of tea and a cosy chat fled, and India rushed across to the double bed, barely noticing the attractive Laura Ashley furnishings and the pleasant ambience of a room which was homely and attractive, rather than glamorous.

Alison was leaning back against the pillows, her face strained and pale, perspiration beading her forehead.

'Alison, are you all right?'

She shook her head, her fingers curling round India's wrist and digging painfully into the soft flesh.

'The baby,' she whispered painfully. 'India, I think something's gone wrong with the baby . . .' She winced as a sudden spasm of pain racked her, biting down hard on her bottom lip. 'Doctor's number in telephone book,' she managed to get out before falling back against the pillows in a dead faint.

To India's relief she found the doctor's number without the slightest difficulty, clearly indexed under 'doctor', and when she rang the surgery number the crisp, efficient tones of the receptionist were immediately reassuring.

'Mrs Taylor, you say?' the woman enquired briskly, clicking her tongue. 'I'll put you through to Dr Jenner—she's his patient.'

There was a second's pause, when India fretted with impatience, not daring to put down the phone to rush upstairs to check on Alison, every second's delay seeming to last a lifetime, but at last she heard the calm unflurried male tones of the doctor, who listened as she explained jerkily what had happened.

'And you say when you arrived she was up a ladder cleaning her windows? These lassies will never learn! I'll be right there. Try to help her to relax . . . Tell her I'm on my way.'

From his accent India guessed that Dr Jenner was from the Border country, and feeling reassured by his calm manner, she replaced the receiver and went back upstairs to Alison.

Her reassurance disappeared the moment she entered the bedroom and saw Alison's still, swollen body, huge mauve shadows under eyes set in a face suddenly far too pale and fragile-looking. India's heart skipped a beat, and all at once she longed for Simon's reassuring presence. Almost went downstairs to ring him, but then she reminded herself that he was in London, possibly in an important meeting, and that nothing could be achieved by alarming him unnecessarily.

It seemed a lifetime before the doctor's mud-stained Ford pulled up outside the front door. India heard the car and rushed to the window, just in time to see a lean, fair-haired man emerging from the car, a battered black bag in one hand as he hurried up the path, his shoulders and back bowed in the perpetual stoop that most medical men seem to pos-sess.

India flew downstairs to let him in, her face nearly as pale as Alison's as she opened the door.

'Aye, well, let's take a look at her, then,' he said to India. 'Silly lassie, I warned her not to have another bairn, but having done so she should have had more sense than to overdo things.'

He seemed to know his way about the house and India remained behind while he went upstairs. He seemed to be gone for an age. When he eventually returned his face was grave.

'I'll have to ring for an ambulance,' he told India briefly. 'She's come into premature labour—still in the first stages, thank God. I warned her she might not be able to carry this child full term. Do you know where we can get in touch with her husband? It might be necessary to operate and we'll need his consent. You'll travel to the hospital with her, I hope; I've given her something to bring her round and she'll be glad of a familiar face when she does.'

As it happened India did know the number of Mel's office in Edinburgh, and offered to ring him, after Dr Jenner had rung for the ambulance, a numbing feeling of unreality enveloping her as she dialled Mel's number. His secretary answered the phone. When India asked for Mel, she enquired who was calling, telling India that Mel was in a meeting.

'I wonder if you can get a message to him,' India began, clutching the receiver. 'His wife . . . She's had to go to hospital—a problem with the baby. Dr Jenner would like him to return home if that's possible,' she added, earning a nod of approval from the doctor, who was filling a hypodermic needle from a phial he had removed from his bag.

'I'll make sure he gets the message,' the girl told India, 'even if I have to interrupt the meeting. Before I go in I'll just check on flight times. May I know who's calling, please?'

India gave her name and rang off.

'Good girl! Now I want your help upstairs,' Dr Jenner told her. 'I want to try and give Alison this injection. It will help to stabilise her condition, and might, with a bit of luck, help to control the contractions until we can get her into hospital.'

Alison came round as Dr Jenner was giving her the injection, looking first at him and then at India, her eyes dark and worried.

'Well, you have been a foolish creature, haven't you?' Dr Jenner told her. 'But don't worry, everything's under control. It was fine lucky for you that this young lady was with you, we'll have you in St Margaret's in two shakes of a lamb's tail.'

'And the baby?'

Dr Jenner had turned away, opening his case deftly to replace the hypodermic, but India was sure she had not imagined the faint pause before he replied, his voice light and reassuring, as he told Alison not to worry about a thing.

Ten minutes later the ambulance arrived, two efficient ambulance men lifting Alison carefully on to a stretcher and carrying her downstairs. When Dr Jenner made to follow them India caught hold of his sleeve, her throat dry with tension as she asked him huskily, 'Will Alison be all right, doctor, and the baby?'

'I don't know. I'm not God, I'm afraid. Alison has a chance, a good chance, but the baby ...' He shook his head, 'It will be just under three months premature—dangerous enough in a young, healthy mother, but Alison is neither of those. St Margaret's has an excellent prem. unit, and the staff there are used to dealing with gynae complications, but in the case where a decision of life or death has to be made ... I hope that girl manages to get through to her husband, and that he gets here soon.'

Nothing more was said, but it was what was left unsaid that lay heavily on India's heart as she followed the stretcher out to the ambulance.

It seemed as though the journey to the hospital would never end, but at last their journey was over and India was trying to keep pace with the stretcher as it was whisked inside and into a lift which bore them upwards to a gleaming, quiet ward. Not until she saw the sign flashing overhead did India realise that they had reached their destination and that Alison was now in the safest and most capable hands.

'I'll get someone to bring you a cup of tea,' the kindly Sister told India.

'But Alison . . .'

'There's nothing you can do for her now,' she was told kindly but firmly. 'Dr Jenner asked me to tell you that all we can do for now is wait. Labour may stop of its own accord. If it does, all well and good.'

'And if it doesn't?' India asked fearfully, but she didn't need to hear the answer. Dr Jenner had already told her that in order to save Alison the ordeal of a protracted and potentially dangerous labour they would have to operate, and that the baby, so very premature, might not survive such an operation, and yet, when she had come round briefly in the ambulance, Alison had reached for India's hand, grasping her fingers to say painfully, 'Don't let them take any risks with the baby, India—promise me. I feel if anything happens to this baby it will mean the end of our marriage.'

Whether Alison was right or not India didn't feel qualified to say, but what she did feel was that if she lost the baby Alison might well turn her back on Mel and give up hope of patching up their differences, and knowing how much she loved her husband India knew that if this were to happen Alison would eventually bitterly regret it.

It was nearly an hour before Dr Jenner came to find her. She had glanced through every magazine in the small waiting room, counted the repeat patterns on the wallpaper and endured such a mental anguish she hoped she would never have to endure such an ordeal again.

'Alison?' India demanded nervously. 'Is she . . .'

'We haven't been able to stop the labour pains,' Dr Jenner told her pragmatically. 'Her blood pressure is rising dangerously, and if her husband doesn't arrive soon, we're going to have to decide whether to operate without his permission.'

'Alison doesn't want to lose the baby,' India told him numbly.

'She has two healthy children who need her more than they need a brother or a sister,' Dr Jenner replied, his eyes softening as he perceived India's white face. 'I'm sorry, lassie, but we have to face facts. Now where is that man of hers?'

It was a question India was asking herself fifteen minutes later when Dr Jenner had just been in to tell her that if Mel didn't arrive within a quarter of an hour they were going to have to go ahead and operate.

He refused to allow India to see Alison, explaining that the drugs she had been given had made her drowsy. 'If you want to do something for her, pray, lassie,' he told India kindly, 'for her and her child.'

That was exactly what India was doing ten minutes later, when the door burst open and a dishevelled Mel rushed into the room, his face set and tight with anxiety.

'Alison?' he demanded urgently. 'How is she? Is she . . .'

'They want to operate,' India told him unsteadily, 'but that may mean that she loses the child, and she's desperate to keep it, Mel.'

'To hell with the baby,' Mel said roughly. 'Alison is more important to me by far.'

'Then perhaps you ought to tell her that,' Dr Jenner suggested softly, opening the door of the small waiting room. 'She's come round and has been asking for you.'

'There's a baggage porters' strike on at Heathrow and I had to charter a plane to get me down here,' Mel explained tersely.

As he disappeared with the doctor, leaving India feeling forlorn and deflated, she could hear him explaining why he had not been able to reach the hospital sooner.

One good thing at least seemed to have come out of the day's events. One look at Mel's strained face had been enough to reassure India how he felt about his wife.

Hours seemed to go by, although in reality it could not have been more than thirty minutes before Mel reappeared.

'They're operating now,' he told India gruffly. 'I've told them that I want Alison safe at all costs.' He dropped down beside India in one of the chairs, his head resting on his hands.

'Oh God, India!' he exclaimed in muffled tones. 'I've been such a crass fool! God, when I think what I've put Alison through. And she's never complained . . . never . . .'

'She loves you,' India told him gently, 'and you love her, even though your love might have gone into hibernation for a while.'

'You're a very nice girl, India Herries,' he told her with a smile. 'And I only hope Simon knows what a treasure he's got for himself. There is one thing I would like to know, though. Were you having an affair with him at the same time . . .'

'I met him for the first time on the day I told you that there was no future for us,' India told him gently. It was after all the truth and would salve Mel's pride while at the same time betraying nothing of the real circumstances of her own marriage.

To her relief before Mel could question her further, a nurse came rushing in looking distinctly harassed.

'Mr Taylor,' she addressed Mel, who got quickly to his feet. 'Come with me, please.'

After that it seemed an eternity to India before Mel returned, but this time his face was wreathed in smiles.

'Alison's fine,' he told India, 'and so's the baby—at least as "fine" as a three-month prem can be. She's in an incubator. They let me look at her—she's so tiny ... but quite a good weight, so they say, and with a pretty fair chance of surviving, especially as she's a girl. They're always stronger.'

'Does Alison know?' India asked him softly.

He shook his head. 'She's still not come round from the anaesthetic. Come on, I'll run you home. You look all in.. Where's Simon, by the way? He can't be too pleased at being deprived of his bride in this way. I must remember to thank him some time.'

'He doesn't know. He's in London—he had to go there last night.' India explained how she had come to be with Alison, and Mel looked grave, shaking his head slightly.

'If you hadn't been there Alison wouldn't have stood a chance. We've both got one hell of a lot to thank you for, India—and not just today. I managed to talk to Alison before they operated, and we've both agreed to put the past behind us and start again.'

'I think you've made the right decision,' India told him gravely.

He had driven from the local airport in a hired car and India relaxed against the headrest, closing her eyes, trying to cast off the dread and tension which seemed to have grown steadily inside her all day.

When they reached the cottage everything was in darkness, with no sign of the Ferrari.

'Simon can't be back yet,' India told Mel.

'I'll see you safely inside, then. And check under the beds, for if you're anything like Alison—she hates going into a dark house.'

'Mmm, I'm not over-keen myself,' India admitted, glad of his protective bulk as he escorted her up the path to the front door, taking her key from her to unlock it and precede her inside, switching on the light as he did so.

'I don't suppose you've got the energy to make me a cup of tea, have you?' he asked hesitantly. 'I haven't had anything since lunchtime—they offered me a drink at the hospital, but I was too strung up to touch it.'

'I could do with one myself,' India admitted, walking into the kitchen and filling the electric kettle.

As an afterthought she opened the fridge and removed half a dozen eggs, breaking them into a bowl and whisking them efficiently.

'Omelettes,' she told Mel when he wandered into the kitchen. 'It won't take a minute and we could both do with something.'

They ate in a companionable silence, each

savouring the relaxation from tension and the knowledge that both Alison and the baby were safe.

'We want to name her after you,' Mel told her. 'It was Alison's idea. She was sure all along that it was going to be a girl, and before they operated she told me that if she ... if she didn't make it and it was a girl she wanted me to call her India.'

India reached impulsively across the table, covering his hand with hers.

'I'm one hell of a lucky guy,' Mel said abruptly, pushing away his plate and standing up. 'Am I allowed to show my appreciation in the time-honoured way?'

India went willingly into his arms, knowing that the brief passionless kiss he pressed upon her forehead was both a goodbye and an acknowledgment that what he had felt for her had been an older man's sudden yearning for youth and all that it represented.

'Friends?'

'Friends,' India agreed, touching her lips to his.

Neither of them heard the front door open, and so both turned in surprise when Simon suddenly strode into the room, his eyes dark and enigmatical as he looked at them, arms round one another, and then at the intimacy of the table set for two, the table lamps the room's only illumination primarily because India had had the beginnings of a headache and hadn't felt up to enduring the more strident overhead lights.

'Surprise, surprise,' he drawled, placing a tissue paper-wrapped bottle on the table. 'Although not quite the one I had in mind,' he added in a self-derisory tone. 'Obviously I ought to have been more considerate and rung to make sure I was expected and welcome.'

'Simon I can explain. You . . .' Mel began.

'No, thanks, Mel,' Simon cut in coolly. 'I'm afraid I'm a great one for letting circumstances speak for themselves. Right now what I'd appreciate most is you leaving my house, and my wife.'

'Simon . . .'

'*Now*, Mel,' Simon said with such iron inflexibility that India said wearily,

'You'd better do as he says, Mel. I'll explain.'

Plainly reluctant to do so, Mel turned on his heel and left them, and not until the front door had closed behind him did Simon say with deadly calm,

'Well, you had me nicely fooled didn't you? What a pity I had to return before the evening reached its ultimate climax. Couldn't you at least have entertained your lover outside my home?'

'Mel isn't my lover,' India said quietly.

'Not yet perhaps,' Simon sneered. 'But obviously it's only a matter of time.'

'I'm not going to attempt to justify myself while you're in this mood,' India said quietly. 'As it happens you've completely misinterpreted the situation . . .'

'Have I?' He reached for her as he spoke, making her wince as he grasped her upper arms with hard fingers.

'We'll see about that, but first perhaps it's time that I showed you what being a wife is all about—who knows, I might be able to kill two birds with one stone. If it's a lover you want, surely I'm as capable of filling that role as my dear cousin-in-law!'

CHAPTER NINE

FACED with the full raging tide of an anger which appalled India with its intensity, she was powerless to prevent Simon from lifting her up in arms which seemed to tighten around her like steel.

At the top of the stairs he kicked open a door—not to the bedroom she had slept in the previous night but his room. It was just as she remembered it from that other occasion, entirely masculine.

'So you thought you could make a fool of me, did you?' Simon demanded thickly as he lowered her on to the bed, pinioning her arms, straddling her so that there was no possibility of escape. 'You underestimated your acting ability—I was so convinced that Mel meant nothing to you that I actually thought . . .' His mouth clamped shut, a muscle working in his jaw, his eyes blazing with a barely suppressed anger that made India cringe in fear. 'And to think I believed that you possessed honesty, decency—even thought that if you did care for Mel, you weren't the sort of woman to steal another's husband!'

'You don't understand,' India began. 'If you would just listen to me . . .'

The sound of his harsh laughter jarred against her already overwrought nerves, her eyes widening in pain as his grip of her wrists tightened.

'Listen? Oh no, the time for listening is over. You're my wife, remember, and as I hate to see a woman frustrated and disappointed . . .'

The sneering mouth closed over her own with smothering violence. India could feel her heart thudding in terror, her body numb with a fear she had never experienced before. This wasn't the same man who had made love to her before, who had said that if they worked at it their marriage must surely have a future. This was a remorseless stranger, bent on destroying every barrier she tried to erect between them, on destroying every last particle of resistance, on humiliating and degrading her, but try as she might India could not avoid the punishing force of that smothering kiss, and to her chagrin, when Simon lifted his head and regarded her with eyes smokey-dark with arousal, for a brief second she felt as though an answering chord had been struck somewhere deep inside herself, causing her body to vibrate against her will to a spell she had no power to resist.

'You try to hide it, but I can tell that you want me,' Simon said broodingly. 'Just as I want you, even though I despise myself for doing so. Forget about Mel,' he advised roughly. 'Forget everything but this, India, because, God help us, it's all there is.'

She tried to stem the wild surge of longing that swamped her at the renewed touch of his lips against hers—not destructively this time, forcing from her a response that grew in depth to meet his own, until there was nothing in the world but the feel of Simon's mouth against her own, his lips invading and exploring, as his hands slid from her wrist, upwards, unfastening the buttons of her blouse and pushing aside her bra to cup and caress the aching fullness of her breasts.

She forgot what had happened downstairs, why he had brought her to this room, reality fading as quickly as frost in the heat of the sun, her whole body turning into a melting, yielding compliance that silently urged his possession.

Clothes were a barrier that tormented and denied. Beneath the fine silk shirt Simon was wearing India could feel the solid muscle of his body, damp with perspiration where it clung to the tanned skin. Remembering the time before when she had performed this task for him, her fingers, unerring, found the small mother-of-pearl buttons, her senses responding instinctively to the warm, musky scent of his body; the feel of the crisp body hair beneath fingers which seemed to have discovered a latent knowledge of pleasure. His flesh against her lips tasted of salt; India felt him shudder deeply as she trailed her fingers lazily down his spine over the strongly formed male hipbone and across the tautly flat stomach which quivered faintly in reaction to her caress, her hand suddenly crushed against him as Simon muttered something unintelligible beneath his breath, his hands gripping her waist as he bent to savour the thrusting hardness of nipples which already ached from the arousing contact with his hair-roughened chest.

Her emotions already aroused beyond the point where it was possible to think clearly or logically, India instinctively sought to prolong the exquisite pleasure, her free hand tangling in the thick darkness of the hair growing low in his nape, her small moan of pleasure echoed by Simon's husky groan.

As though her body's response to his caress had

swept away all her natural restraints, she could only delight in Simon's thorough and prolonged exploration of her body, each fresh wave of pleasure delighting and startling her with its intensity and drawing an instinctively answering caress from her own fingers as they stroked delicately over skin which covered hard bone and muscle like a layer of oiled silk. Lost in the wonder and mystery of discovering that a man's body could be so truly beautiful, India was conscious of nothing and no one but the man holding her against the aroused warmth of his body while teaching hers the exact meaning of the verb 'to pleasure'.

When his lips grazed the satin-soft skin of her stomach she shivered ecstatically, her eyes closing on a wave of yielding desire and need, which found a brief but unassuaging appeasement as Simon parted her thighs with his knee. Opening her eyes momentarily, India had a brief impression of the tanned, dark maleness of his thigh against hers, sprinkled with dark hairs, taut with a strain she could also see etched in his face, and then his lips were against hers, his arms tightening round her as she felt the full thrusting power of his desire.

'I won't hurt you this time ... I promise you,' India heard him say, but the words reached her as though she were in a dream; the fear of pain had never been farther from her mind, her entire body was urging her towards a fulfilment she could only guess at but which promised appeasement and cessation of the deep ache which arched her against Simon, her nails digging into the smooth flesh of his back, her small plaintive cries silenced beneath his mouth as her unspoken plea was answered, a delirious, singing pleasure taking her far beyond pain, beyond anything but the complete rightness of Simon's possession, the ultimate oneness of being part of a deeply loved person. And then there was no room for thought, only the waves of pleasure crashing down over her, carrying her far, far out to sea, and then back to a sunwarmed beach where her body could lie in absolute peace . . .

India opened her eyes slowly, recollection filtering back, her eyes widening and turning to the pillow next to hers as full remembrance of the evening's events swept over her.

The other side of the bed was empty, the only sign that it had ever been occupied the dent in the pillow.

She felt strangely reluctant to move, a delicious and hitherto unexperienced lethargy making her give in to the desire to simply remain where she was, allowing the birdsong outside and the bright sunlight to wash over her.

The house itself seemed strangely quiet, and at length, when curiosity overcame her lassitude, India left the bed and padded into the bathroom, averting her eyes from the sight of clothes—hers and Simon's—strewn haphazardly on the floor, a mute reminder of how desire had swept everything else aside. And yet on her part not simply desire, but love; the deepest, most womanly part of her had responded to Simon like a flower opening out to the sun, drawing from her a response which she knew instinctively she would never experience with anyone else. He desired her, Simon had said; and she had known that he spoke the truth, but desire was not love, and in Simon's case she doubted if he would even have desired her had he not thought she had planned to let Mel become her lover. It had been as though the finding of the two of them together had sparked off an anger in Simon so deep that it had pushed aside everything but the need to assuage that anger in the most primitive and effective manner possible.

And yet she could not entirely regret what had happened. It had proved if nothing else that Simon wanted her, and perhaps in time . . .

But first she would have to convince him that she and Mel had been together entirely innocently. Somehow . . .

The thought of Mel reminded India of Alison and the baby. Dressing quickly, she ran downstairs. There was no sign of Simon, nor of his car, and a cold finger of fear touched her heart. Where was he? Telling herself not to be stupid, she dialled the number of the hospital. Alison and the baby were both doing fine, she was told. Hanging up, India tried Mel's home, but there was no reply. He was probably on his way to the hospital, she reflected, wishing she knew where Simon had gone and why— Was he perhaps regretting last night? Or worse, had she somehow betrayed to him how she felt? A marriage based on hopeless love on one partner's side and pity on the other's could never succeed, and suddenly it had become very important to her that their marriage did survive. If she wanted it to she would have to cultivate a careful façade; allowing herself to respond just so much and no more. She bit her lip, wondering perhaps if Simon, still believing the worst of Mel's presence in the house, had perhaps gone back to London.

It was almost lunchtime before she heard a car draw up outside, and running to the living room window, saw Simon emerging from the Ferrari. There was nothing to be read from his expression which was, if anything, withdrawn and shuttered.

She had spent the morning tidying up and had prepared a casserole lunch on the offchance that Simon might return. The rich meaty smell of it infiltrated the hall as she opened the door, and for a moment neither she nor Simon said anything, merely looking at one another. Against her will India felt her colour rise, her pulses racing as she dragged her eyes away from his jean-clad thighs, trying not to remember the contrast between his dark skin and her fair one. Simon was casually dressed in jeans, a checked woollen shirt, and a slate blue leather jacket.

'Something smells good,' he commented, taking off the jacket.

'It's only a casserole,' India said hesitantly. 'I wasn't sure . . . that is . . .'

'You thought I might have gone to demand satisfaction from Mel in the time-honoured tradition?'

No such thought had crossed India's mind, and she looked uncertainly at him, determined to tell him the truth before there could be any more misunderstandings.

'Simon . . .' she began, but he let her get no further, interrupting,

'I need a drink. Let's go into the living room and sit down.'

India noticed that he poured himself a generous measure of whisky without diluting it, but she shook her head when he asked if she wanted to join him.

'No vices,' he said, grimacing slightly, 'unlike myself. It seems I owe both you and Mel an apology. I went to see him this morning—primarily to tell him that there was simply no way I was going to allow him to have an affair with my wife. I'd got it all planned, right down to telling him exactly how you'd responded to me, if he got stubborn, but it wasn't necessary. All he could talk about was Alison and the new baby, and how marvellous you'd been.' He had his back to India, and was staring out of the window, so it was impossible for her to see his face, or to guess at what he was thinking behind the cool mask of his voice.

She went towards him hesitantly, reaching upwards to touch his arm. He withdrew from her as though her touch had burned, an expression in his eyes that turned India's heart to stone. He hates me, she thought wearily, loathes me, can't bear me to touch him . . .

A sick helplessness rose up inside her, leaving her unable to do anything but retreat into the chair she had been occupying before, while Simon continued jerkily, 'God knows I've done some crassly stupid things in my time, but this . . .'

'You mean our marriage?' India asked, trying to appear calm.

'Among other things.'

'We could always separate . . .'

'Have you forgotten why we got married in the first place?' Simon demanded sardonically, glancing significantly over her slight slender body. 'And there's even more reason now, not less. No, we stay together, but to ensure that there's no repeat of last night, it might be as well if I stayed in London for a while—alone.'

He wasn't looking at her, but India could still feel the warm flush rising up under her skin. What was he saying? That he had guessed how she felt about him and that to avoid any embarrassment—for either of them—he thought it best that he didn't place any temptation in her way. And there would have been temptation, she admitted painfully, knowing that she could not easily have endured knowing that he was sleeping in the room next to her.

'But if I promised,' she began unsteadily, casting pride to the winds, determined not to let him go without a fight, because she foresaw that if he returned to London and left her here alone it would mean the end of all her hopes that eventually Simon might come to care for her. He didn't want to care for her, she admitted honestly. He wanted to preserve the distance between them and she cursed herself for being foolish enough to betray to him how she felt, convinced that it had been her passionate response to his lovemaking which was making him have second thoughts.

'Words dictate promises,' he told her harshly, 'but emotions dictate actions.'

Meaning that she would not be able to keep hers, India thought drearily, and it was probably true.

'If you're sure it's for the best,' she said emotionlessly.

'For the best? God knows. The best thing would have been for us never to meet, but we have done; and we're both aware of the consequences, and I won't condemn any child, never mind my own, to the bitter rejection that comes from not having a father.'

'And if there is no child?' India asked quietly, remembering how, just after their wedding, he had said they could make a go of their marriage no matter what—but of course, that had been before he realised that she loved him. It was one thing proposing a marriage between two sensible adults, but quite another when one of those adults had to carry the burden of the other's love.

'We'll be let off the hook,' he said curtly.

There seemed nothing else India could say. Simon left shortly after lunch and she yearned to be able to reach out and touch him, to kiss the hard line of his mouth.

'When will you be back?' she asked him as he threw his case into the boot of the Ferrari.

'I don't know.'

It was the end of a brief dream. Her most sensible course now was to pray that she wasn't pregnant, India told herself, but strangely enough she found herself stubbornly praying for exactly the opposite. One half of her writhed in self-contempt, but the other refused to give up the fight, even when she told it that there was no point in going on.

At the end of the week Alison returned home from hospital. She telephoned India to report progress on the baby, who was thriving in the premature unit of the hospital, but would not be allowed to go home until she had reached a target weight of six pounds. As she was barely three this was obviously going to be some time.

'But at least she's healthy,' Alison told India cheerfully. 'And I have you to thank for that. Mel is over the moon. He's always wanted a daughter. Simon came to see me while I was in hospital. He seemed very withdrawn. Is everything all right, India?'

'Fine,' she lied cheerfully. 'He's rather busy at the moment and has been staying in London.'

'Aha, so that's the reason for it! Obviously he's missing you. Why didn't you go with him?'

'Oh, I've been feeling a bit tired lately,' India fibbed.

'Umm—well, if you'll take my advice—and remember I've been through it, so I am speaking from experience—you'll get him home just as fast as you can. To men like Simon and Mel, work is an important part of their lives—in fact I almost lost Mel to it, so don't make the same mistakes I did, India. Be at your husband's side, not away from it.'

'Don't worry about us. Tell me more about the baby.'

Alison was easy to divert, and it was half an hour before India was able to replace the telephone receiver. She had been spending her afternoons during the week working on plans for Meadow's End. Simon hadn't said whether she was to continue or not, but she had doggedly gone ahead, telling herself that if she had no faith in the future what hope was there.

Two days after Simon's departure for London, a brand new, shiny estate car had been delivered to the house—something she would need, Simon had told her when he rang up to see if it had been delivered, and while she had been overwhelmed by his generosity she had also been chilled by his cool reception of her thanks. He had rung her from the flat and in the distance she had been able to hear music and the chink of glasses as though he were not alone, but rather than stoop to jealous questionings she had said nothing, and the estate car had proved extremely useful for her forays into Bristol and Gloucester to investigate the shops. She wanted to keep Meadow's End as authentic as possible and had, with the aid of a list published by the National Trust, found a firm who specialised in interiors, and furnishings which were exact replicas of those produced in the past. India already had her own ideas, but she was reluctant to crystallise them until she had spoken with Simon, and somehow the telephone was not the ideal means of discussing her plans.

When she had finished speaking to Alison she decided to go into Gloucester to do some shopping. Simon might return for the weekend and she had nothing very exciting in the fridge.

It was a fifteen-mile drive, and when she got there she parked the car and headed for her favourite food store, pausing now and again to study the displays in sundry dress shop windows. Jenny had been keeping her up to date with everything that was happening at the salon, but very soon she was going to have to a make a decision about her future and that of the business. Officially she was having a month's holiday, which she could well afford to take, because most of their orders were well in hand and if any crisis did arise Jenny knew that she was only a phone call away.

It was while 'India was studying one of the windows that a familiar female voice hailed her. She spun round, surprised to be confronted by Ursula Blanchard, clad in an elegant black suit, her hair and make-up flawless.

'Dear me, the little bride, and window shopping too. How dreary! Shall I give Simon your love when I see him tonight?'

Somehow India managed to keep her face rigid, even managing to force a smile past stiff lips, as she said coolly, 'Don't bother, it's something I prefer to do in private.'

She could tell by the momentary flash of rage in Ursula's eyes that she had scored a hit, but her triumph was shortlived when the other woman said with acid sweetness, 'But not very often, surely? Simon hasn't been home in a week, has he.'

It was a statement rather than a question, and India felt the nausea churning like bile in her stomach.

'He's taking me out to dinner,' Ursula continued blithely, 'and then afterwards we're going on to a new club. I shouldn't be at all surprised if we don't see the sun rise together—it used to be one of our favourite pleasures,' she added meaningfully. 'You're out of your depth, my dear. Simon is not the man to be entertained for long by inexperience or doting adoration. I've told him that sometimes it's necessary to be cruel to be kind, but he's a man who prefers the subtle approach—you know what I mean? Those little telltale things that tell a woman silently but clearly that she's no longer wanted . . .'

'As he did to you?' India asked, fighting not to let Ursula get the better of her, but it was a losing battle and they both knew it. She writhed in self-torment, imagining Simon telling Ursula about the circumstances of their marriage.

'Of course,' Ursula added insincerely, 'Simon has a

ridiculously chivalrous side to his nature as well, but I feel sorry for the type of woman who clings pathetically to a man who no longer wants her, knowing that he's too compassionate to shake her off, don't you?'

She was gone before India could retaliate, and, her shopping forgotten, she walked slowly back to where she had parked the car.

That Ursula was speaking from selfish motives India did not for one moment doubt, but she also knew that the only reason Simon was continuing with their travesty of a marriage was because he thought she might be carrying his child, and because of his own childhood he could not bear to desert his son or daughter, but he did not want *her*. Or at least, India amended, not permanently.

The house felt cold when she got back. Even though they were well into spring it was still very cold. She turned on the radio just in time to hear a news bulletin that snow might be expected before evening. There was then a discussion involving two weathermen and an expert on changing climatic conditions, all trying to explain exactly why the seasons appeared to have become so muddled up.

By late afternoon India was shivering and decided to switch on the central heating, but for some reason the mechanism refused to respond. She rang the service number indicated on the panel, but was told by a harassed receptionist that only emergency calls were being dealt with and that she would be put on what was apparently an extremely long list.

In order to keep warm she lit the living room fire with some logs she found in the garage, and added an extra sweater and thicker pantyhose under her jeans for extra protection. It was cold in the kitchen, so she made do with a supper of toast and coffee, eaten huddled over the fire.

At just after seven o'clock the snow came, not pretty, fluffy flakes, but driving, blinding whiteness which hurled itself malevolently at the windows and clung tenaciously to the ground. Within half an hour everything was white. The temperature seemed to have stabilised, but India could feel her body heat starting to drain away with the enforced inactivity. The fire was burning low, and as she saw that the blizzard was showing no signs of blowing itself out she bitterly regretted not continuing with her planned shopping. Apart from the basic necessities and sundry tinned foods, there was literally nothing in the house. She had no experience of driving in snow and ice, and could only pray that the morning would bring a thaw.

CHAPTER TEN

IT didn't. India, who had slept downstairs, to keep warm, wrapped in the quilt off her bed, awoke to a world of blinding whiteness, where the sun shone brightly out of a cold blue sky on to the snow which had been driven by the fierce wind and now lay piled in huge drifts over the drive and the road beyond it. Nothing moved in a landscape that was all white and blue, and it was an eerie sensation which made India shiver as she stared disbelievingly

out on to a landscape of which she seemed to be the
only living inhabitant.

The blizzard must have affected their supply of
electricity, India realised when she went into the
kitchen and waited in vain for the kettle to boil. The
house felt cold, the central heating system refusing
to respond to her tentative manipulation, the telephone was completely dead when she picked up the
receiver. Forcing down the panic which had filled
her at the knowledge that she was completely alone,
cut off from the outside world in a house which was
gradually growing colder and colder, India battled to
control the primitive fear racing through her. There
was an open fireplace in the living room. She could
light that; there was wood and coal in the garage. He
liked an open fire, Simon had told her, and upstairs
there was a radio alarm clock which ran off batteries.
She raced upstairs, switching it on quickly, relief flooding through her as she heard the sound of a D.J.
announcing a record, the sound of another human
voice restoring a little of her normal self control.

The snow would melt, she reassured herself. Her
imprisonment would not last very long. She had
food, the means of providing herself with warmth and
the radio for company, what more could she want?

As though by doing so she could keep at bay the
fear which attacked her every time she glanced out
of a window and saw the still, alien landscape
beyond it, India forced herself to wash and dress,
piling on extra layers of clothes to protect herself
from the cold which seemed to seep deeper into her
body with every breath she took. Only when this
task was completed did she allow herself to think
about her meeting with Ursula. Simon didn't want

her. That was something she had to face—but not now, a tiny voice pleaded, not now.

Despite the fire she had managed to light the living room seemed to grow colder and colder. The temperature was well below freezing, and would drop even further, the radio weatherman announced, following a news bulletin during which India learned that vast areas of the country were cut off and isolated by the unexpected blizzard. People were warned not to attempt to travel along motorways blocked by huge drifts of snow, and in country areas food was being dropped by helicopter for those animals who had managed to survive the storm. Electricity supplies were cut off in many areas, and no firm promises could be given as to when they would be restored. People were warned to stay inside and keep warm, and India shivered as she heard this last item. Despite her endeavours, despite her extra layers of clothing her teeth were chattering with every breath she took, her body chilled to the bone. But worse than her physical discomfort was the knowledge that she was not carrying Simon's child. This last blow had destroyed her last fragile hope that she might be able to save their marriage. If there was to be no child, there was no possible reason for the marriage to continue.

She wanted to cry, but somehow the tears would not come. She was too cold, too tired, numbed by the terrible coldness which seemed to have invaded every part of her body.

During the late afternoon it snowed again and then froze, a thin crescent moon shining down from a midnight blue sky, the silver illumination of the moon and stars glittering on the white brilliance of

the snow. India drifted into an uneasy sleep, punc-
tuated by nightmares wherein she was constantly
trying to reach Simon—a Simon who remained elu-
sively just out of reach, surveying her with that same
sardonic indifference he had shown at their first
meeting. She cried out protestingly in her sleep,
begging him to listen to her, to wait for her, but
always just when she was about to reach out for him
he turned on his heel, Ursula's heartless laughter
filling the silence.

India awoke, reality and fantasy merging in her
cold-numbed brain, until she was sure of nothing
save for the fact that she had lost Simon; and with
him all reason for living. Never had she envisaged
feeling like this; experiencing this tearing sense of
loss, of hopelessness, of desire to turn her back on the
world and simply slide into oblivion.

Simon, Simon, her aching heart called, while her
tired brain yearned simply for peace, for escape from
pain and hurt.

She slept and dreamed, dragged out of her cold-
induced sleep occasionally by a body too young and
full of life to simply submit without a fight.
Occasionally reality managed to break through and
India would come to with a start, shivering and
acutely conscious of her danger. The fire had gone
out. There was wood still and coal in the garage,
but she simply lacked the will to go and get it. What
was the point? She had lost Simon, without him life
held no meaning, no purpose.

Coward, an inner voice mocked her, but she
refused to listen; it was much easier simply to curl
up into a small ball and pull the quilt round her,
letting sleep claim her.

Someone was shaking her, rubbing agonising life into numbed limbs, the stabbing red-hot needles and pins torturing her flesh and dragging her back from the endless sleep reaching out for her. She mumbled a protest, curling herself into a small ball, trying to avoid contact with whatever it was that was inflicting the unwanted pain on her body.

'India ... wake up! Open your eyes!'

Responding instinctively to the calm authority in the voice calling her name, India's eyelids flickered, her eyes focusing slowly on the taut male features, the mouth set hard in a grim line, the dark blue eyes, almost black in their anger. A deep shudder racked through her, causing Simon's hands to cease in their ministrations to her cramped limbs.

'India—no, don't close your eyes. Wake up! Drink this ...'

Fiery spirit trickled down her throat, forcing her back to life in spite of her protests.

This time when she opened her eyes she focused them properly.

'Simon!' His name whispered disbelievingly past her lips. What was Simon doing here? He should be with Ursula. Ursula was the one he loved. India had no rights to him. The child which might have held them together was not to be. These and other muddled thoughts flashed through India's cold-numbed brain, while her senses struggled to relay to her the fact of Simon's presence, his hands rubbing briskly at her near frozen legs, his dark head bent towards her, while he muttered something un-intelligible under his breath.

'Why didn't you light the fire?'

'I did,' she told him, shivering fitfully, longing to

close her eyes and blot out his angry face. She had been asleep and comfortable. He had woken her from that sleep, making her aware of cold, aching bones, and a pain that seemed to go on and on for ever. 'It went out. Simon, I'm cold, I want to sleep. Leave me alone.'

India was barely aware of uttering the words, unaware too of the look which crossed her husband's face, before it settled into lines of grim determination and he bent, scooping her up and carrying her effortlessly over to the settee, where he wrapped her in the quilt before turning his attention to the fire.

It was the noisy crackling of burning logs that woke India, her forehead furrowed as she tried to recall events that were no more than vague, hazy images. She was aware of someone coming between her and the fire, and she shivered at being cut off from this source of heat.

'India, I know you're awake. Open your eyes!'

Unwillingly she did as Simon commanded. What was he doing here? Why wasn't he with Ursula?

'How did you . . .'

'. . . get here?' she had been about to ask before exhaustion robbed her of the strength to frame the words, but Simon obviously misunderstood her because he said tersely, 'How did I know you were here? Jenny rang me. She'd heard about the weather conditions on the news and she was concerned about you.'

There was something contained within the words that India knew was important, but which eluded her, some discrepancy which she knew she ought to question, but she was too tired and cold to do so.

Her teeth started chattering together. She heard Simon curse and saw him move towards her. 'You ought to be in hospital, but I daren't risk moving you yet. You must try to stay awake, India. It's important. You're suffering from hypothermia—you know what that is, don't you?'

She managed to nod her head, wishing she had the courage to tell him to go away and leave her. She had been quite happy, drifting away on a peaceful cloud, but he had come and wrenched her back from that dream world, into another filled with harsh realities; a world where she was forced to acknowledge her love for him and the folly of it.

'Ursula,' she managed to murmur painfully, watching him frown with misery in her heart.

'I've brought some Calor gas with me and a small stove. I'm going to heat up some soup for both of us . . .'

Simon disappeared and India closed her eyes, shaken out of her lethargy what seemed to be only seconds later when he returned, cursing angrily as his fingers tightened round her upper arms, shaking her into unwanted consciousness.

When he was sure that she was awake he connected the cylinder of gas to a small portable stove, deftly opening a tin of soup which he poured into a pan.

'How did you get here?' India asked him hesitantly, glancing towards the window. Although dusk was gathering outside she could still see the snow-covered landscape, and could remember the size of the drifts covering the drive and the road.

'Land Rover,' Simon told her briefly, not telling her how hazardous the journey had been and the sheer impossibility of transporting her in her present state to the hospital care she so obviously needed. He frowned as he poured a generous helping of the soup into a bowl and handed it to her.

India drank it without enthusiasm. Pins and needles attacked her legs and feet whenever she moved. She felt so cold that she could not imagine ever being warm enough ever again. When she had finished the soup Simon handed her a glass of brandy, telling her to drink it. She obeyed him docilely, unable to find the energy to defy him even though she hated the taste of the liquid as it brought burning life to her throat and stomach. However, the soup and brandy combined together to make her more aware of her surroundings, of what had happened to her, of the fact that Simon was no longer under any obligation towards her. She opened her mouth to tell him so, but Simon himself was already on his feet, removing the protection of the quilt and staring down at her with a frown in his eyes.

'You're half frozen.'

It was a statement, not a question, and as such did not need an answer. Besides, India's body spoke for her, shivering with reaction at the removal of the quilt. Simon dropped the quilt back over her and turned on his heel, leaving the room without a word. It was beyond India to guess at his thoughts. The soup and the warmth of the fire had revived her to the point where she could think with reasonable clarity, but despite the flames licking so greedily at the stacked logs none of their heat seemed able to reach out and melt the ice which seemed to have invaded her body.

When Simon came back he was carrying an armful of bedclothes which he deposited on the floor in front of the fire, while India watched him, unable to comprehend the reason for the grim purposefulness she could read in his eyes.

Not even when he came across to her, removing the quilt and lifting her bodily in his arms, did she realise what he had in mind. It was only when he placed her on her side on the makeshift bed, with her back to the warming flames, that he spoke, his words causing a chill far greater than that she was already experiencing to tremble through her body.

'Sleep together?' Her eyes mirrored her shock. 'But . . .' But I can't—you don't love me, she had been about to say, but Simon cut short her protests, anger igniting in the depths of his eyes as he said curtly,

'No buts, India.' His mouth turned down at the corners, a cynical expression twisting his lips as he added coolly, 'My motives are purely altruistic, believe me, and motivated by a desire to keep you alive rather than a desire for your body.'

India could well believe it. She opened her mouth to tell him that she knew he didn't desire her and that it was to preserve her own self-respect that she had tried to turn down his suggestion, but Simon had his back to her, and was already removing the thick sweater he had been wearing.

This was madness, India told herself, touching her tongue to lips suddenly dry with a tension which began somewhere deep down inside her, curling crampingly through her stomach and tensing all her nerve endings, as she watched Simon remove the checked woollen shirt he had been wearing beneath his sweater. In the firelight his skin gleamed bronze, shadowed by the dark hair across his chest, as he turned suddenly, and she veiled her eyes, not wanting him to see the desire she knew must be mirrored there.

All the instincts which had been subdued by her hypothermia suddenly came leaping to life, her brain sending warning signals flashing the length of her body, telling her just what humiliation and self-betrayal she courted if she allowed Simon to carry out his intentions. She hadn't been aware that he was watching her until he said suddenly, in a voice gritty with anger,

'For God's sake, India, don't make this any harder for us both. If it helps think of me as a stranger; think of this as the only means of preserving both our lives.'

She tried to, closing her eyes against the images flickering between her and the fire, the knowledge that this was Simon's body touching her own, Simon's hands that removed her clothes and brought her icy flesh into almost painful contact with the warmth of his. It was necessary, he told her, feeling her tense; their shared body heat would give her the strength to make the dangerous journey back with him in the Land Rover, and she had nothing to fear from him, nothing at all.

It wasn't him she feared, India longed to tell him, but herself; her body's traitorous response to the proximity of his; her own suffocating longing to reach out and touch him, to trace the shape and feel of him with fingers suddenly restored to painful life.

The hopelessness of her love overwhelmed her. While she was having to command every ounce of self-control she possessed to stop herself pleading with Simon to make love to her, he was as composed as though they were the strangers he had referred to earlier. Lying on her side, trying desperately to preserve the small distance between them, India was convinced that she would never, as Simon instructed, sleep. She was shaken with alternate waves of desire and self-contempt, so fierce that they left her trembling with reaction. Unlike her Simon seemed to have no trouble in sleeping. She could hear his deep, even breathing. He moved, his arm coming out to curve her against him, her breasts pressed against the warmth of his chest, and panic seized her. She was torn between twin desires, equally powerful, one telling her to move away while she still had the will-power, the other urging her to take advantage of the opportunity fate had given her, telling her that the memory of these moments in Simon's arms would be something to gloat over in the long, lonely years ahead. Simon muttered something in his sleep, his hand cupping her breast, and the decision was made for her. Closing her eyes, India allowed herself to dream that Simon held her out of love and not merely necessity, that the touch of his fingers against her breast was born of desire for her rather than an automatic response to the femaleness of her body.

India felt deliciously warm, protected; still hazy with sleep, she stretched, then stiffened suddenly, her eyes flying open. Simon was still asleep, his features relaxed and curiously vulnerable. Impelled by a desire stronger than her will to resist it, India ran her fingers lightly over his face, tracing the shape of his bones, an aching love for him welling up inside her. He opened his eyes and for a moment both of them were completely still.

'India . . .' His lips formed her name, his breath grazing her skin as he bent his head towards her.

Her lips parted instinctively as his touched them, her breath released on a sigh as Simon's hands stroked over her body, holding her against him, his lips exploring the shape of her mouth and then its hidden inner sweetness.

India wanted the kiss never to end. It transported her beyond the boundaries of reality into the realms of fantasy where everything was possible, even that Simon could love her. She closed her eyes, her fingers digging into the hard muscles of Simon's back, losing herself in passionate response to him, arching her body against him in a tangible invitation that needed no words.

For a moment she thought he was going to respond, and then suddenly like a douche of cold water he thrust her away, his eyes brilliant with anger as he stared down at her.

Humiliation washed over her. How could she have been so lacking in self-respect, so caught up in her own desire as to forget how Simon felt about her? Shaken with self-revulsion, she turned away, closing her eyes in an attempt to blot out the memory of his anger-darkened eyes and pressure-whitened fingers as he clamped them round her wrists to force her away.

'Stay where you are. I'll get dressed and see what the weather's like. With any luck we should be able to leave now you're feeling stronger.'

No mention of what had just happened, of how she had betrayed herself. She ought to be glad that he had prevented her from humiliating herself still further, India told herself as she heard him move about the room, throwing fresh logs on the fire and walking over to the window, pulling back the curtains, but all she could feel was a vast, welling sense of deprivation, a longing to be held in his arms, to be touched and caressed with a desire that matched her own.

Instead she forced herself to ask if the weather had improved enough for them to be able to leave. For a moment Simon was silent and then he turned towards her, his face a grim mask, an unfathomable expression in his eyes as he said curtly, 'Improved or not, we're leaving. Somehow I don't think it would be in either of our interests not to, do you?'

Her face burning, India sought desperately for the reply that would convince him that her desire had sprung from no more than a momentary reaction to his maleness, but she couldn't find the words.

Sick at heart, she watched him prepare their breakfast, forcing herself to drink the soup she didn't want, her throat aching with suppressed tears and tension.

When Simon went outside to the Land Rover India dressed. Her body no longer felt cold, but on fire, burning with shame and self-contempt. What kind of woman was she? How Simon must despise her! Hadn't his earlier words proved that he did? Hadn't he said that he would rather risk the snow and ice than remain alone with her?

Simon insisted on carrying her out to the Land Rover. India lay unmoving in his arms, shuddering as an icy wind burned into her exposed face.

The Land Rover was not built for comfort. It was

cold and draughty, and sitting inside it, India could well understand why Simon had not wanted to risk travelling in it before. That he had saved her from death she did not doubt; nor did she doubt that he had been right to insist on sharing with her the life-restoring heat of his own body, but how she wished he had not.

It took them three hours to drive the brief distance to a main road which had been partially cleared by a snow-plough. Twice Simon had to stop to dig them out of packed snow, and although India had offered to help he had refused to let her do so.

When they reached London Simon insisted on taking her to hospital, to check that she was suffering from no after-effects of her exposure to the cold, and although she wanted to refuse, India lacked the will-power to be able to do so.

A kind but firm nurse took charge of her in the casualty department. She was not the only person to be brought in suffering from the cold, she told India as she deftly helped her to undress and passed her a hospital gown. The wards were crowded with victims of the blizzard.

'Don't worry about your husband. You'll be able to see him once the doctor has checked you out,' she told India, not knowing the reason for the shudder which racked through her patient's frame at the mention of Simon.

Perhaps it was better this way, India thought tiredly as she was led to a ward and tucked up in bed. This way Simon could walk out of her life without the indignity of her losing her self-control and begging him to stay. Where was her pride? Her determination never to let her heart rule her head?

She felt the tiny prick of a needle and then sleep began to steal over her, blotting out the past and the future, and she submitted to its welcome oblivion, glad of the opportunity to escape from her bitter thoughts.

The doctor who examined India told her that she had been lucky. Another twenty-four hours in the conditions she had endured prior to Simon's arrival and she would not have survived.

And he called that 'lucky', India thought wryly. How little he knew!

'In fact by tomorrow you'll be able to go home,' the doctor continued briskly. 'I've already told your husband he can come and collect you in the morning.'

Like an unwanted parcel, India thought drearily, trying to imagine how Simon had reacted to the doctor's information. If she had any self-respect she would simply discharge herself and go home to her own flat, thus relieving Simon of the burden of wondering what to do about her. Their marriage was over. If Ursula's words had not confirmed it, Simon's actions when he thrust her away from him had done so—more effectively than any amount of words.

Perhaps because the nursing staff were so busy, India found it relatively easy to discharge herself. After all, she was a relatively healthy young woman, whereas many of the victims of the blizzard were old people who had suffered far more seriously than she had.

Her flat seemed empty and lonely after the bustling busyness of the hospital. To dispel her depression India tried to make herself busy, forcing herself to make plans for a future in which she no longer had any real interest.

After making herself a light supper she tried to concentrate on some work, but the images which took shape under her pencil were not of clothes, but of Simon—Simon smiling, Simon frowning; Simon . . . India pushed away her sketches tiredly. What was the use of dwelling on the past? Her ordeal had taken more out of her than she had thought. By nine o'clock she was ready for bed. What would be Simon's reaction in the morning when he went to collect her from the hospital? Relief?

She was just stepping out of the bath when she heard her doorbell ring. Grabbing a robe, she went to answer it, falling back in dismay as she opened the door and saw Simon standing there. He took advantage of her surprise to walk into the hall, slamming the door behind him, the brief action revealing to India the fury betrayed by the anger gleaming in his eyes, tension in every line of his lean body.

'Just what the hell do you think you're playing at?' he snarled before India could speak, his fingers fastening on her upper arm with complete disregard for her still damp flesh. 'What are you trying to do to me, India?'

'Do?' She stared at him in bewilderment, sickness churning in her stomach as she realised that he had completely misinterpreted her actions, and must have thought that she had deliberately tried to force him into coming to see her by her premature flight. Taking a deep breath, she steadied herself, willing herself not to give way to her emotions.

'There's no need for our marriage to continue,

Simon,' she told him bravely, her head dropping so that she wasn't forced to witness the relief in his eyes. 'I'm not . . . I'm not having your child.'

For a moment she thought he couldn't have understood her, so complete was the silence, and then with an oath that brought her eyes to his face in startled disbelief, India felt his fingers tighten into her arms, his teeth gritted in fury as he said softly, 'Oh, you're not, are you? Well then, perhaps this time I'll damn well have to make sure that you are!'

This totally incomprehensible statement was followed by another brief curse, a muscle jerking spasmodically in his jaw, as Simon used his superior strength to force her backwards into the hall, before he swung her off her feet, carrying her into her bedroom. There was no time for her to protest. The brief protection of her robe was torn ruthlessly from her as Simon released her to study her body in a thick silence.

'Come here.'

It wasn't possible for her to ignore the hoarse command. India moved towards him like a sleepwalker, unconscious of her nudity, drawn by the glittering darkness of the eyes which swept her like iron to a magnet.

'You're my wife,' Simon told her thickly when she reached him, 'and I'm getting tired of playing games.'

His hands stroked over her body as he spoke, arousing all the feelings she had been trying so hard to suppress.

'Simon . . .'

As though her voice broke a spell, Simon groaned suddenly, reaching for her.

'Don't speak,' he told her tautly, 'don't say anything. Let me look at you.'

He held her away from him, while his eyes moved hungrily over her body, and India trembled, caught between amazement and disbelief. Why had he come to her like this? Simply because she was his wife? She dared not ask him; dared not risk breaking the spell which seemed to hold them both in thrall.

Simon's eyes glittered strangely as they moved over her, a subtle tension filling the space between them, growing with every passing second.

'India . . .'

He breathed her name against her mouth, filling her senses with the scent and taste of him as he lifted her and carried her to the bed. An aching urgency took possession of her, a desire to obliterate everything but the reality of his presence, for whatever the reason.

In the darkness he ran his hands over her body, stroking and caressing, his tongue painting erotic circles against her breast as India tugged impatiently at his shirt buttons.

His mouth against her breast triggered off a wave of emotion she was powerless to deny, her soft, panting cries inciting him to demonstrate to her that the feeling she was experiencing was but the tip of a sensual iceberg.

His skin felt hot and dry against her own, and India was overcome by a desire to cradle him against her. He wanted her, and surely she had every right to encourage him to allow her body to melt into total yielding enticement against the growing demand of his thighs. Her mouth was dry, her heart beating suffocatingly fast. She wanted desperately to be part of him, to be possessed by him, and yet some inner voice cried out to her to stop while she still had some measure of self-respect. She tried to ignore it, but it refused to be silenced. Her body tensed in Simon's arms, his lips ceasing their assault against her skin.

'What's the matter?' he demanded.

'I can't,' India told him. 'I can't, Simon—not without love.'

His curse made her wince, as did his grip of her arms as he pulled her against him, letting her feel his own arousal, his eyes burning with a need he made no attempt to disguise. For a moment India thought he was going to ignore her, and then with a groan he released her, levering himself off the bed and starting to dress.

'You'll have to forgive me,' he said wryly as he pulled on his jeans. 'I promise you I don't make a habit of forcing women to submit to me—but then I've never been in love before.' He turned to look at her. 'When I got to the hospital and found that you'd discharged yourself I nearly lost my mind. I couldn't understand why, when you'd endured my suspicions and jealousy, you should choose to leave me now. That's why I came round here, to demand the truth.' His lips twisted in a bitter smile. 'It never occurred to me that it was because you'd discovered you weren't to have my child.'

'But that was the only reason you married me,' India interjected. 'Because . . .'

Simon laughed harshly with self-mockery, coming to stand beside her. 'Let's get one thing straight,' he told her. 'I married you for one reason and one only—because I'd fallen deeply in love with you.

God, you must have known,' he demanded when India stared up at him. 'That night, after we'd been out to dinner with Alison, surely you knew . . .'

'Knew what?' India asked him in a voice that trembled slightly. 'All I knew was that you seemed to hate me because you thought I was trying to take Mel away from Alison, and then when you . . . when we . . .' she stumbled over the words and fell silent, leaving Simon to say curtly,

'When I all but raped you, isn't that what you're trying to say?'

'You didn't know . . . you thought . . .'

'I didn't know that you were a virgin?' Simon demanded huskily. 'That didn't make any difference to the way I felt about you, India, except to fill me with gut-wrenching shame because I'd turned what could have been a beautiful experience for both of us into a travesty of what it should have been, simply because I'd been too blinded by jealousy of Mel to see past what I'd thought of as the "facts" to the truth behind them. And even that I turned to my own advantage, forcing you into marriage, telling myself that I'd make you love me. Only it didn't work out that way . . . and still I haven't learned my lesson. I came here tonight, telling myself that I couldn't let you go.' He got up as he spoke, tiredness, and something else—an emotion which sent the blood thudding through India's veins—clearly visible in his features before he turned towards the door.

'I'll make arrangements for the divorce.' He had almost reached the door. Another moment and he'd be gone, and still India didn't know what to say, how to convince him how she felt. She tried to speak, her throat tight, as she thrust back the bedclothes and padded after him.

'Simon . . .'

He turned and saw her, pain darkening his eyes, as he warned, 'India . . .'

'Aren't you going to kiss me goodbye?' India knew she was playing with fire, but she could think of no other way; there was no other way. She walked towards him. He was as motionless as a statue carved from stone, only his eyes alive and full of a pain which made her heart ache in response.

'India, for God's sake don't do this,' he warned hoarsely, and then he was touching her, running his hands over her body like a blind man seeking to impress its image into his perpetual darkness, and India was drowning in the waves of pleasure shuddering through her, her lips against his throat, feeling the pain with which he drew breath into tortured lungs, only to expel it in a protest which turned to a smothered groan as she ran her fingers lightly over his chest, lifting his hand to the aching fullness of her breast, her breath catching in her throat as she said huskily, 'Please, Simon, don't leave me. I need you. I love you . . .'

For a few seconds she thought he wasn't going to believe her. Tears shimmered in her eyes as a fear that she had imagined his declaration of love for her filled her, and then she was gathered against him, his mouth coaxing her lips to part with a sweet urgency that compelled her to lock her hands behind his neck and give herself up completely to his kiss.

It was a long time before he released her.

'Why didn't you tell me before?' he demanded huskily at last.

'Why didn't you tell me?' India countered. 'I didn't know you loved me. I hoped we might be able to build a life together, but then you accused me of wanting to take Mel as my lover . . .'

'Sheer jealously,' Simon admitted ruefully. 'I'd gone from thinking you completely lost to me as Mel's mistress, to disbelieving hope that as you were nothing of the kind I might have a chance of winning your love, only to be plunged down into abject despair by discovering you both in what, you have to admit, were unencouraging circumstances. I masked my fear that I'd lost you by telling myself that you'd deceived me all along and that you really wanted Mel . . . in fact I think I went a little mad with jealousy.'

'I wanted you,' India admitted softly, blushing slightly. 'Right from the start.' She frowned suddenly, remembering something. 'But you left me . . .'

'Because I couldn't endure staying with you and not being able to do this . . . and this,' Simon told her, tracing a line of tender kisses from her throat to her lips. 'Can't you understand, India, I had to leave you or completely lose my self-respect; I couldn't stay in the same house as you and not make love to you,' he finished simply.

'But Ursula told me you loved her, that you wanted me to leave . . . that was why . . .'

'Ursula!' Simon's eyes darkened. 'She seems to have been very busy lately. I ran into her in London one day and she told me that she'd seen you in Gloucester and that you'd told her that you were returning to London—leaving me. That was why I didn't go down to Meadow's End the moment the weather turned bad. It wasn't until Jenny rang me to ask if I knew where you were because she hadn't been able to get in touch with you that I realised the truth. I tried to ring the house and when I discovered that the line was out of order, I came down as fast as I could, only to find you almost on the point of death.'

In order to banish the tense, haunted expression from his eyes, India raised herself on tiptoe, running her tongue lightly over his lips, her eyes coaxing him to forget what was past.

'You were so cold, so clinical and uncaring,' she told him softly. 'I couldn't endure it when you held me in your arms as though I were simply a stranger in need of care and attention. You were so distant.'

'Distant!' Simon grimaced slightly. 'Have you any idea of what it cost me in willpower to behave as though you were a stranger? Of what it was like trying to sleep with your body next to mine, knowing that I had only to reach out to touch you?'

'I felt the same,' India admitted. 'When I woke up you were still asleep, and then you woke up and . . .'

'And I had the devil's own job not to take you in my arms and make love to you there and then,' Simon finished grimly. 'That's what I'd descended to; even knowing how dangerously close you'd come to succumbing to hypothermia, how weak you still were, I still wanted you—desperately.'

There was a moment's silence while each remembered their separate pain, and then India said softly, 'I'm not suffering from hypothermia now, but I do need to feel you close to me, Simon.'

'You do?' He was smiling as he spoke, lifting her

high in his arms, his heart thudding rapidly against her cheek as he carried her across to the bed.

She reached up for him, her heart in her eyes, as she saw the love shining out of his.

'Love me,' he whispered as his lips claimed hers. 'Love me, India, because I don't think I could bear it if you didn't.'

'I do,' she told him huskily, letting her body tell him, without the necessity of words, the intensity of her love for him, and receiving in return reaffirmation of his softly spoken words of love.

The past and all its unhappiness slid away. The future stretched gloriously before them, but for now India was more than content with the present, here in Simon's arms, his body teaching her the true meaning of the pledges he had just given her.

AN INNOVATIVE YOUNG DESIGNER

India, the heroine of Penny Jordan's Presents, is a dress designer. And as such she is following in the illustrious footsteps of the innovative British designers of the sixties and seventies—a classic example of whom is Mary Quant.

Mary Quant studied art and fashion at London University's Goldsmith's College, and after graduation worked for two years as a hat designer with a popular Danish milliner. But her first love was dress designing, and in 1957 she opened a small clothing store in Chelsea—one of the most fashionable areas in London. That store, Bazaar, was an overnight success. The first dress store to be known as a boutique, it was the favorite haunt of fashion-conscious young women from all over London.

Quant quickly became known throughout Europe and North America as a uniquely trend-setting young designer; her distinctive trademark, a white five-petaled daisy, was displayed on all her creations—from dresses to cosmetics. By the early sixties young fashion designers and hairdressers were flocking to London to study her ideas. Vidal Sassoon opened his first hairdressing salon on London's Bond Street, and there invented, especially for Mary Quant, the classic "geometric" cut. "Swinging London" became the center of the fashion world, and Quant-designed mini-skirts and -dresses were seen everywhere. The voluminous, long-skirted styles of the fifties were "out," and simple, abbreviated, functional clothes were definitely "in."

Mary Quant single-handedly transformed the fashion scene. Her clothes were exciting, unusual, wearable and above all accessible. Exclusive high fashion was exclusive no longer!

SUPERROMANCE

Longer, exciting, sensuous and dramatic!

Fascinating love stories that will hold
you in their magical spell till the last page
is turned!

Now's your chance to discover the earlier
books in this exciting series. Choose from
the great selection on the following page!

Choose from this list of great

SUPERROMANCES!

SUPERROMANCE

Complete and mail this coupon today!
